T0356420

HORIZON

WALKING ON EGGSHELLS

JENNIFER PHILLIPS

Book design by Karli Kruse
Cover design by Karli Kruse
Photographs on pages 156–159 from Shutterstock Images

Published in the United States by Jolly Fish Press, an imprint of North Star Editions, Inc.

This is a work of fiction. Names, characters, places, and incidents are either the product of the author's imagination or are used fictitiously, and any resemblance to actual persons living or dead, business establishments, events, or locales is entirely coincidental.

Library of Congress Cataloging-in-Publication Data
Names: Phillips, Jennifer, 1962- author.
Title: Walking on eggshells / Jennifer Phillips.
Description: Mendota Heights, Minnesota: Jolly Fish Press, 2025. | Series: Horizon | Audience: Grades 10–12.
Identifiers: LCCN 2024035778 (print) | LCCN 2024035779 (ebook) | ISBN 9781631639128 (hardcover) | ISBN 9781631639135 (paperback) | ISBN 9781631639142 (pdf) | ISBN 9781631639159 (ebook)
Subjects: CYAC: Cooking--Fiction. | Psychoses--Fiction. | Family life--Fiction. | Friendship--Fiction. | Multiracial families--Fiction. | LCGFT: Novels.
Classification: LCC PZ7.1.P5238 Wal 2025 (print) | LCC PZ7.1.P5238 (ebook) | DDC [Fic]--dc23
LC record available at https://lccn.loc.gov/2024035778
LC ebook record available at https://lccn.loc.gov/2024035779

Jolly Fish Press
North Star Editions, Inc.
2297 Waters Drive
Mendota Heights, MN 55120
www.jollyfishpress.com

Printed in the United States of America

WALKING ON EGGSHELLS

JENNIFER PHILLIPS

JOLLY
FiSH
PRESS

Mendota Heights, Minnesota

CHAPTER 1

I'm not sure where to put the shiny white plastic bag with its hard handles. The bag is stuffed with proof that I just went through a life-crushing kick in the teeth. Discharge paperwork. Contact details about appointments I promised to keep. Prescriptions my dad has to get from the pharmacy right away. A flyer reminding me of the crisis hotline in bold black numbers. A half-finished toothpaste tube I threw in as a "souvenir."

Dad shrugs when I hold the bag up. He's exhausted. Because of me.

He finally points to the dining table. "I'll sort through it later. Your aunt and uncle are stopping by. Then I'll go get the meds. Are you hungry? Or do you want to shower first?"

My turn to shrug. I'm exhausted too. But here I am, back home like I wanted. It feels good. But weird. Quiet. *So* quiet after three weeks on the psych ward. And private.

Only me and Dad instead of a unit filled with people dealing with their own private hells in front of each other and the staff.

"Kai?" Dad asks. "You okay?"

I drop the bag on the table and smile so he'll think I'm okay. So he won't pick up on the mix of fear, worry, and panic holding my insides hostage. I gave the feeling a name in the hospital. Grippy. A nod to the inside joke among some of us on the ward about how we're taking a grippy sock vacation. Sometimes Grippy stays in the background. But he can take over quickly.

"I put your room back together," Dad says. "The way you like it."

That makes no sense. "What was wrong with it?"

"Well, I guess you don't remember. It got a little messed up as you got sicker."

Grippy gives me a jab. What else happened that I don't remember?

Dad moves in to give me a hug. I'm not up for that right now, so I head into the kitchen.

I find the ingredients for yakisoba in the fridge. I need to eat. One of the new meds makes me hungry all the time. At least I love to eat. And cook.

Crap. My hands shake so hard I can't open the noodles. Dad notices and takes the packet to help me. He slides his hand on top of mine and squeezes.

"Breathe, Kai Kai. You've got this."

I do what he says. Big breaths, in and out. That gets me through setting up the cutting board to slice the carrots, cabbage, and green onions.

I jump when the front door bangs open. The knife nicks my finger.

"Watch your back," the man whispers. "Not sure it's safe here."

Only I hear the man. So I've been told. He's in my head, even though he sounds like he's standing right over my shoulder. It's a crap situation. But I can't just order him to leave me alone.

Soft arms hug me from behind, and kisses tickle my scalp.

"Hi, Serena," I say, relaxing.

"Sweet boy. I'm so glad you're home."

My auntie sees the blood seeping from my cut and wets a paper towel to press on it. "I help make the meal, yeah? Just this time."

I let her take the knife and finish prepping. She won't make it the way I like. But my brain is in slow motion, and I'm starving.

Dad and Uncle Lonny talk in low voices in the living room. About me, although I'm supposed to pretend I don't know that. I hear Dad give a quiet "no." Then Lonny rounds the corner and moves in for a hug. He holds me tight, like he's trying to squeeze the pain out of me. Dad looks at his brother and sister. They've got stuff they want to say. Oh boy.

"Go ahead," Lonny tells him, releasing me. "It's the right thing."

"So," Dad starts. "We're wondering if you want to let your mom know what's going on."

Whoa. I didn't expect this. She's been out of the picture

since I was small. I know Dad's in touch with her sometimes. But he doesn't share what they talk about.

"Why?" I ask, dizzy with hunger. Serena whisks together soy sauce, sesame oil, and other ingredients. I grab a banana from the counter.

"She always asks how you're doing," Dad says. "I think she'd want to know."

Lonny gets plates and cups from the cabinet. "And there's another reason. Go on, Felix."

Dad sighs. "I haven't mentioned this to you before. But your mom had a psychotic break too. A long time ago. Maybe she can help. You know, be someone who's been through it, who can understand."

Wow. They did *not* just unload that piece of shocking news on me. The cramped kitchen suddenly feels impossibly small. It's too crowded with my smothering Chinese-Hawaiian family. I escape to the living room without answering and curl up on the couch.

They talk over each other, debating whether to follow or leave me alone.

"We can talk about it more later, Kai," my dad calls out. I don't answer.

So my mom lost her mind too. Small detail my dad forgot to share over the years.

I wonder what her breakdown was like. And is she still dealing with this stuff now? Maybe that's why she moved away. And stays away. My mom and I don't talk. I don't know why they think that would change. Not sure I want to talk to her anyway. And about this? No way.

"Let's eat," Serena says as she leans over the couch and rubs my shoulder.

I only notice the uncomfortable silence after I've shoved down a plate of yakisoba. It doesn't have that special flavor I coax out of my recipe. But I'm so hungry it doesn't matter. They look at me like I dropped from another planet. A messy, starving, shaky alien. That's fine. Fits how I feel.

"Good chow, Auntie," I say, sitting on my hands to control the shaking. Another fun med side effect.

"Not as good as yours, I know," Serena says, smiling. "You teach me, eh?"

Lonny nudges a plate of cut-up oranges my way.

"Your dad says the hospital suggested you spend time in a special outpatient program to keep feeling better," he says. "What's that called again?"

"It's an intensive early intervention program," Dad says. "It helps people who've had a first psychotic episode adjust. Makes sure they're feeling stable and ready to move forward."

They stare at me and wait. Apparently, they want a response.

"You remember them talking about that?" Dad asks gently when I don't answer.

"They talked about a lot of things," I say. "I'm good. Just want to rest and get back to normal."

"Us too, Kai," Lonny says. "Us too. But this stuff is tricky. I've seen it with other people. This program would help make sure you're ready before you jump back in to school. And ready for your job training at the restaurant."

Or I could land back in the hospital if the program people don't like what they see. That's my big fear. But I can't tell them that. I'm under the microscope now. Any wrong move and my family could put me back in the hospital.

I can't take them talking at me. But I can't take nervous silence either.

"I'm going to take a shower and lie down for a bit." I put away my dirty dishes and slip out the other side of the kitchen. Their low voices fade as I head to my room.

It's been weeks since I've been alone. I ease the door to my room shut and hope they'll forget I'm here. The sweet silence washes over me. Everything's in its place: neat, clean, in order. My control room. Dad said he put it back this way. That I'd messed it up. It's scary not remembering. People telling you something is not the same as remembering it yourself. Or maybe he said that to make my episode sound worse than it was?

Not being sure what's real—that's the hard part. But it's early days. The doctors said the meds will take time to kick in.

My phone's on its charger on my desk. Do my friends

know I'm home? Are there messages waiting? And how's that reunion going to go? I unlock the phone and get ready to face the world again.

CHAPTER 2

I wind through our neighborhood of houses with small fences and neat yards. It's pushing ninety degrees in our mountain town. Everyone's at work or inside with their window ACs running. That spares me having to make small talk with any neighbors. I can imagine how that would go. No thanks.

My armpits are soaked by the time I reach the park. My flip-flops don't protect my feet from the brittle grass that's turned the color of wheat.

My friends are gathered at a covered picnic table, putting out food and paper plates.

"I can do this," I mutter to myself as I walk up. "Breathe, breathe, breathe."

Ian sees me first. "Lummy!" he calls.

Gavin and Josie add their own "Lummy!" cries.

I smile. At least I think I'm smiling. I hope I am.

Josie pulls me into a hug that pins my arms to my sides. The top of her head barely reaches my neck.

"Missed you," she says.

Gavin gives me a shoulder squeeze.

Ian lightly punches my arm. That makes me jump back.

"Sorry. Didn't mean to startle you," he says. A look flashes among all of them. Their radars are up, trying to detect any changes in me.

I shake it off. "I'm good."

Josie grabs the grocery bag from my hand. "What is this? You did not bring ordinary food from the deli. We were looking forward to a Kai Lum signature dish."

I don't want to tell them that my foggy brain isn't cooperating in the kitchen. "Sorry. No time to cook. Lukewarm chicken legs for you today."

We finish setting out the food and fill our plates. If they notice my shaking hands, they pretend they don't.

After talk about the food dies out, the obvious topic hangs in the air. But no one's sure how to bring it up. Including me. I focus on emptying my plate.

"Our school schedules post tomorrow," Gavin finally says.

Josie takes a bite of my chicken, leans close, and makes a silly it's-so-good face. After she swallows, she says, "I hope they don't have me running back and forth across campus like last year. I could barely get in a pee break between classes."

Time to ease into things, I guess. I take a deep breath. "I'm going to school with my dad tomorrow. We need to talk with the staff. Make sure there's a plan in case I need help. And I'll have to swing by the nurse's office at lunch each day for one of my meds."

Ian slides another of his grandma's extra-spicy tamales onto my plate as I talk. He keeps his eyes on me. He's always been the one in our group who's not afraid to ask the direct questions.

"How are you feeling, Kai?"

Breathe, breathe, breathe.

I shrug. "Why? I'm better now. Don't I look okay?"

"No, you look better," he says quickly. "Just wondering if, you know, you want to talk about it."

"Your call," Gavin adds. "Either way, we've got your back."

I sit on my hands and try to settle down my bouncing legs.

"I guess I'm better," I say. "The meds make me feel weird though."

Josie leans against my arm. I'm not sure I can handle the tears in her eyes.

"We were so scared for you," she says. "We didn't know what to do. How to help you."

This is my chance to fill in the gaps in my memory. To know what happened. I hope I can handle that. Either way, I need to know.

"What went down at the festival?" I ask. "I mean, I know what they told me at the hospital. But things are blurry. You were there."

"What's the last thing you remember?" Gavin asks, watching me closely.

What do I remember? Honestly, most of the summer is gone from my mind. Only bits and pieces float by. I'm not sure what's real.

I remember feeling so full of energy that I couldn't sleep, but it didn't matter because I didn't want to sleep. Feeling annoyed when Dad didn't want to hear my ideas about opening my own culinary school someday. Panicking because a guy I couldn't see kept talking to me.

"Kai? You okay?" Ian leans over the table to put his hand on my forehead. It's an old joke. He's always wanted to be a doctor. Any little thing we have going on, he checks our temperature.

I force a smile. "Yeah. Trying to figure out what I remember."

Grippy gnaws at me. I scoop some mixed fruit onto my plate.

"We were listening to that one band. Some guy was hassling me," I say slowly, pushing the fruit around my plate. "And the music was so loud it was crushing my head. I tried to leave, but some people wouldn't let me go. They kept saying I had to stay so the music could calm me down. But I really wanted to get away from the sounds. I remember riding in a van. I didn't realize that I had been taken to a hospital until a few days later."

My friends are quiet. Too quiet.

"Well?" I ask. I shift uncomfortably.

Birds swarm our group as Gavin sweeps crumbs to the ground. "The music was bothering you. But you were already rambling when you showed up. We were actually trying to get you to leave with us. But then you started screaming at the band. You said they were trying to kill everybody by releasing a poisonous gas through their music."

I feel like puking. "Did anyone from school see? Are they talking about me?"

They all look at each other. Do they think I can't handle their answer?

"Truth," I demand.

"Yeah," Josie says. "But not just because of the festival. You'd been acting weird for weeks. Sometimes saying things that didn't make sense. Getting really pissed off at people about nothing. Looking a mess, not dressed all neat like you usually are. We kept asking why you were so stressed."

"I should have figured out you were getting sick," Dr. Ian says. "What did the hospital say? Did they give you a diagnosis?"

Can I really trust them?

"Between us, right?" I ask, holding up my fist. I get a bump of agreement from each of my friends.

I take a deep breath. "They called it a first episode of psychosis. And they think I'm bipolar."

I can't look at their faces. "But it's early days," I say, mimicking my doctor's voice. "First, we stabilize. Then we learn to manage the symptoms."

No one talks. Not sure what to say, I guess. And what can they say? It sucks, and I have to deal with it.

"And to make things weirder, turns out my mom has bipolar too," I share.

That startles them.

"Whoa," Josie says. "How did this come out?"

"After I got home. I think my uncle pressured my dad into telling me."

It gets quiet again.

Gavin breaks the silence. "Well, at least you won't miss any school. That's good, right?"

Ian and Josie add their agreement.

"Yeah, I need to stay on track with the job training at the bistro," I say. "The doctors want me to do some full-time outpatient program for now. But I'm not messing with my culinary schedule."

We pack up our food and throw away the trash.

"What happens if you don't do that program?" Josie asks as we leave the park. "You take meds and what else?"

"I do regular clinic visits. Try to not let stress trigger any symptoms. And get back to normal."

"Will it go away?" Gavin asks. "Like, is it curable?"

The question smacks me in the face. Is it? Things have been so upside-down, I never asked.

I shrug. "Don't know yet."

"No worries," he says. "One step at a time, right?"

We head our separate ways at the edge of the park.

One step at a time. Guess that's the best I can do for now.

CHAPTER 3

Dad knocks at my bedroom door. "I'm done with the yard work. Wanna watch an episode or two of *Chopped*?" He's taken the day off work so we can meet with some of the school staff.

"Sure. Be out in a bit," I call.

I hit the replay button to hear my song again. It's got a slow jazzy beat and a melody that soothes me.

I move from my desk to my bed to the closet to the window. And then I walk the same path again. Over and over. The pattern helps with the twitchiness poking at my insides.

I need calm today. Who knows what the school's going to say. What if they treat me like I have some kind of contagious disease?

Two more run-throughs of the song, then I go find Dad. He turns on the TV, and we settle on the couch together.

The *Chopped* chefs open a basket with oysters, edible flowers, pickles, and hibiscus tea.

"Well?" Dad asks, smiling at me.

I try to come up with ideas using those ingredients. Months ago, I could have tossed out ideas rapid-fire. Now, my brain's scrambled.

"I'd do something fancy with the oysters. Use a squirt of pickle juice instead of lemon juice," I try. "And maybe do a hibiscus vinaigrette for a side salad that includes the flowers."

"That could work," Dad says.

We watch the chefs run for ingredients.

"So, you sure you want to do this?" Dad asks during a commercial break.

"Cook?" I ask. "You know I do."

Dad nudges me with his elbow. "No, I meant school. Going there today and getting set up to go back. I still think online school is a good option. For the fall semester, at least."

Grippy gets tighter. My body flips to full alert.

"I can't miss the culinary training program. You know that. I have to go back."

"Maybe they'd let you do that program in person and the rest of your subjects online," he says. "We can ask."

He's been talking with Hunter, my therapist. I can tell. They're plotting this, trying to keep me away from school.

"I need to get back to normal!" The words explode out of me.

Dad gets up from the couch and starts straightening the living room. He's stressed. He always cleans when he's stressed. "No need to yell. Okay, let's talk to them about it all today. I'm worried it's too soon. And I'm worried about how other kids might treat you."

"Don't trust him," the man warns. I shake away the voice. Dad cares about me.

"I know," I say, trying to control my temper. I need him to understand. "But the gossip will be worse if I disappear for a whole semester. Think about that."

Dad sighs and sits on the other side of the couch. He stares at the TV, but I can tell he's not really watching the show. We missed how it worked out with the first set of ingredients. I'll have to replay this episode later.

Afterward, Dad grabs a folder with some paperwork about me and we head to school. A talk show plays on the car radio to an audience of no one. We're both in our own heads with our own worries.

The vibe changes when we walk into the school's common area. The open space where everyone watches everyone. I had hoped there wouldn't be too many kids around yet. But there are. Maybe for sports or clubs starting up. Or to do their own meetings with teachers.

The laughing and chatter die down. I keep my hands in my pockets so no one can see them shaking. They think I don't notice their stealthy looks and nudges while we walk by.

We find the school psychologist's office quickly. I've seen Mr. Brown around school, but we've never had a reason to meet. He's got a small computer table that he can slide up or down to stand or sit. When we come in, he's sitting on a big green exercise ball, typing away.

Dad shakes his hand and gives him the paperwork. The school nurse appears in the doorway.

"Hey, Krissie," Mr. Brown says. "Have you met Kai Lum yet? And this is his dad, Felix."

Krissie shakes Dad's hand and gives my upper arm a squeeze. I've been to her office a few times over the years. A fever that turned into the flu. A finger that got smashed in a door. A panic attack I couldn't explain.

Mr. Brown gestures for us to sit.

"So, Kai, this is a chance for us to talk about what will help you as you start school again," he says. "Your dad brought me up to speed on where you're at with outpatient treatment. How are you feeling about coming back?"

"Don't listen to my dad. I'm ready," I say. "I'll be fine."

Dad shifts in his seat and sighs. Mr. Brown rolls back and forth on his green ball. "What am I not listening to your dad about?"

"He wants me to do online school. But I got into the culinary job training program. I can't miss that."

"Yes, I've heard about your cooking skills," he says,

giving me a big smile. "I can't wait to sample your dishes one day."

"I'm worried it will be too stressful and he'll get sick again," Dad says. I grit my teeth. Why won't he listen to me?

Mr. Brown looks over the paperwork and hands it to Krissie. Then he turns back to me.

"What do you think about your dad's worry?" he asks. "The school district is used to working out flexible arrangements when kids need them. We can look at a variety of options."

This is it. They get what they want. Screw what I want.

"The doctors cleared me to come home," I say. "I don't want to do online."

They all glance at each other. Maybe I got a little loud. I clasp my fingers together in my lap.

"I need to stay in culinary arts and do the job training," I explain.

"Okay, let's think through accommodations we should put in place," Mr. Brown says after a moment. "Are there specific triggers that can bring on symptoms, for example?

Or maybe ways we should adjust your schedule so you're not pushing yourself? Warning signs that you're getting out of your baseline? Those kinds of things."

I can only shrug. The last few months are a blur. And all of this stuff is like learning a new language. I can't keep up.

Mr. Brown looks at Dad for answers.

Dad chooses his words carefully. "Well, I'll be paying closer attention now for symptoms, like him saying things that aren't clear. Or that don't seem to match the facts of a situation. That would be something for his teachers to note too."

Krissie flips through the forms. "It looks like you'll have a lunchtime med to take, right?"

"Yeah. How does that work?" I ask.

"Your dad will bring us a supply that we'll keep locked up," she says with a smile. "You can come by during your lunch period to take it. One of us is always there."

I hate this.

"Maybe I don't need that dose?" I glance at Dad. "What if I just do morning and night?"

Dad's face creases into a map of worry lines. "The medication is keeping you stable. We can't mess with the dosage without talking to Dr. Chu."

Krissie takes notes on the form.

"I get how you feel, Kai," she says. "But I have kids that come to my office to take meds for all kinds of medical conditions. No one will know exactly why you're swinging by."

That makes me laugh. "They all know. Everyone knows what happened."

Mr. Brown pulls up a file on his computer. "Then let's get a plan in place. And also, know you can always come here or to Krissie's office if you feel overwhelmed. I mean that. We want you to show up."

"What are you going to tell my teachers?" I ask. "I don't want Mrs. Rosembert to see something that makes her change her mind about me."

"They'll get a copy of the plan we make so they can support you," Mr. Brown says. "Do you want me to talk with Mrs. Rosembert about your concerns?"

Do I? Will that help? Or will it make it seem like a bigger deal?

"I'll talk to her," I say. That buys me a little time to figure this out.

I feel better as we leave Mr. Brown's office after the meeting ends. Dad doesn't look like he feels better though. They didn't take his side and try to convince me to not come back in person. It doesn't help when he hears two students whisper about me as we walk by. Maybe it's good I'm getting a taste of the attention now. There's less mystery about what to expect in a couple of weeks when school starts.

CHAPTER 4

On the first day of classes, my phone buzzes with texts. I try to concentrate on the group chat without bumping into anything on my walk to school. At least the heat broke and I'm not being broiled like a steak.

Ian: *Meet at usual spot before class?*

Josie: *Can't. Got biology all the way across campus*

Me: *Boo. Well, I'm almost there*

Gavin: *I can do a quick sec*

Josie: *Bummed I don't have classes with any of you this year*

Ian: *We'll meet at lunch then, don't be late*

Me: *I'll come after my mandatory visit to the nurse torture chamber*

Gavin: *Krissie's cool*

Ian: *First class, Lummy?*

Me: *History. Mrs. Galano*

Josie: *I've got her in the afternoon. We can compare*

Gavin: *Here we go. 11th grade!*

I'm still head down, deep in the conversation, when I walk into the school. Not thinking. Not ready with my guard up. Then I look up.

The harsh reality of the rumor mill smacks me in the face. Some kids stare. Some try to sneak looks. It's like there's a spotlight shining on me. I'm today's curiosity. The shy kid who went crazy this summer.

Did you hear? Were you there? Why is he back? Is he safe?

It's hard to know what I'm really hearing and what I'm imagining. I rush toward our meeting spot at the back of the commons.

It's a relief when I finally spot Ian and Gavin. They stand out in the crowd, both tall and lean with dark hair. I hurry toward them.

They notice the attention I'm getting. It's impossible not to notice.

"You okay?" Gavin asks when I stop next to them.

I can only shrug. I wanted to come back. I knew it would be like this.

"I think it'll only last a day or two," Ian says. "Then they'll move on to some new drama. Hang in there."

I nod and take a few deep breaths. Gavin and Ian talk about the star football player who was suspended over the summer. They try to guess what he did and when he'll be back.

I can't really follow what they're saying. The noise from excited kids vibrates through the building and into my brain. I jump when a girl shrieks nearby. She's only laughing, caught up in a funny story with her friends. But my heart races.

"Hey, Lummy. Take it easy," Ian says.

Gavin touches my elbow. He looks concerned. They both do. "Sure you want to do this?"

I take another deep breath and force a smile. "Yeah. I'll be okay. It's just a lot for my senses at first."

We take off for class when the first bell rings.

Kids pour down the network of hallways. I've known many of them since elementary school. Always been on friendly terms. Has my episode destroyed that? I get uncomfortable head nods from some. No one talks to me. Are they avoiding me? Or are they lost in their own heads? It's hard to tell.

US History is torture. I sit in the back and hide my shaking hands. Mrs. Galano seems nice enough though. She's determined to make the class interesting. She talks and talks and talks. Her words flow around me like water around a rock. Nothing sinks in.

"Boring stuff," the man says.

I look around, even though I know where the man is.

World Lit is next. It's too loud in the hallway. Kids are packed tight. It's impossible to not run into each other. The hallway noise hums and buzzes and rattles in my head. I need to break free. This isn't safe.

"Hey, Kai," a boy yells over the heads of some kids. "Have a good summer?"

This catches me off guard. I recognize him from one of

last year's classes. Can't remember his name. Is he making fun of me? Or is he out of the loop?

"Hey," I say. "I'm good. What's your next class?"

"Trig." He waves as the stream of students carries him into a different hallway.

World Lit is the same as US History. But at least the man leaves me alone.

I'm exhausted by the time I make it to the nurse's office at lunch. I slip in and hope no other students noticed. That's probably a lost cause.

"Good to see you again, Kai," Krissie says when she looks up.

I feel like a shaky mess and can't steady my breathing. At least no one else is here yet. No prying eyes.

She motions for me to sit. "The first day can be a lot for anyone. Actually, the first week or two."

I sit and try to calm my body while Krissie gets my lunchtime med from a locked cabinet. The walls have all of the official memos and warnings she has to post. But surrounding those are funny cartoons and quotes about nursing, school, and life. I concentrate on them instead of the feelings inside me.

Keep calm and let the school nurse handle it.

I became a school nurse for the fame and money!

Life is what happens when your cell phone is charging.

Leave homework to the last day because you'll be older and wiser.

"How were classes?" she asks.

"Sweet as honey," I reply.

That makes her snort. "Or sour as old kimchi?"

That makes *me* snort. Grippy relaxes his clutch on my gut a bit. Maybe Gavin's right and she is cool. She doesn't look that old. And she doesn't put off that fake friendly vibe that some grown-ups do when they don't know how to act around teens.

"Any triggers yet?" she asks as she hands me the pill and a small cup of water.

"The noise. It's so loud," I say. Wait. That came out too fast. Who knows if I can trust her. I need to be careful. "Not a big deal though."

She studies me for a long moment. I force my breathing to slow.

"Yeah, I'd love to have magic powers that silence some of your classmates," she says. "I mean, there's regular noise. And then there's annoying noise. Right?"

That makes me snort again. "I bet I know who you're thinking of."

"I'll never tell," she says with a sly smile. "Okay, off to lunch with you. And hang in there. Remember that the first days will feel rocky. Any strategies you've learned that could help?"

I think about that. "Keeping my mind on something specific. Maybe that could help block out some of the noise."

"Good idea. Let me know how it works. But come see me if it gets to be too much, okay? I mean that."

I nod and leave her office. That wasn't too bad.

I find Ian, Josie, and Gavin at our usual spot.

"What's with the big grin?" Josie asks me.

"Nothing. Thinking of some funny stuff," I say. I've been

running through jokes in my head since leaving the nurse's office.

She scoots over, and I sit on the bench next to her. "I think biology is going to be a piece of cake," she says.

"For you, sure," Ian says. "It may kill me." He tugs her blond ponytail, and she twists his arm behind his back before he can react. Josie's trained in self-defense. She's got pure muscle packed in her tiny body.

They watch as I take my lunch out of my backpack.

"Better be something good, bro," Gavin says.

But my Spam musubi looks sad. The seaweed wrap is wrinkled, and the rice could be packed tighter. I also couldn't remember my secret sauce recipe. I try not to let that get to me.

"Not my best work," I explain. "I'm still getting my mojo back."

"Better than anything we could do," Ian says.

We talk about our classes, other kids, how we're going to survive nine months of school. The usual stuff. Normal, like I hoped. I start to relax.

We compare our rotating schedules. Meeting for lunch will be harder this year. "Let's make it happen whenever we can, okay?" Josie asks.

We all fist-bump our promise.

"Wanna do something later this afternoon?" Gavin asks me. Josie and Ian have part-time jobs after school this year.

"Not today. I'm meeting with Mrs. Rosembert," I tell him.

She's been my cooking teacher since ninth grade. She helped me apply for the job training program I'll do this year on top of her class. I need to know for sure that she hasn't changed her mind about me.

"Earth to Kai." Josie squeezes my arm. I flinch. "Sorry! Just bringing you out of your head," she says.

She, Ian, and Gavin have packed up. They start heading to their classes.

"Let me know how your meeting goes," Gavin calls. "But Mrs. Rosembert will have your back. I know it."

Will she? Or will she be too worried about whether I can do it? I don't even know the answer to that. *Can* I do it?

Grippy's angsty feeling spreads through my body again. There's no way I'm going to follow anything said in classes this afternoon.

CHAPTER 5

The sound of clanging pots and pans drifts into the hallway as I reach the culinary classroom. I stop outside to take deep breaths and get my brain to focus. I'm a wreck, but I can't show it.

Mrs. Rosembert is organizing the room when I step inside.

"Yoda?" I call, falling into our familiar dynamic.

She spies me in the doorway and smiles. "Grasshopper. I've been waiting for you."

The rhythm of her Haitian accent always takes my anxiety down a notch.

"Come," she says. "Help me get everything ready. First class was the young'uns. You remember what a mess you made at the start?"

I toss down my backpack and follow her lead, putting

cookware where I know she wants it. We work in silence for a few minutes.

"I wish I'd known about you getting sick this summer," she finally says. "I would have called. And visited if you were up for that."

I didn't realize she cared about me that much. I turn the other way and straighten the spices so she can't see how this hits me.

"Now I realize why you were acting differently in the spring," she continues. "I would have said something if I'd put two and two together."

"What do you mean?" I ask, looking back. "What was I doing?"

She motions for me to help her rearrange some tables.

"You looked so edgy and hyper. You started getting upset over the littlest of things. And sometimes you mixed things up." She smiles gently. "I remember how one day, you said were going to candy the onions and sweat the orange peel. I was like, 'What is he talking about?'"

"I remember feeling weird," I admit. "But I had no clue why."

"I thought it was end-of-school-year fatigue. But . . ." She looks at me. "Do you want a cup of tea?"

I love her ginger tea. I nod, and we get that brewing. When it's done, we perch on stools at the stainless steel kitchen counter.

"Mr. Brown told me how much you want to keep on track with the training program. I'm not worried about my class," she says, waving her hand. "I can adjust things and keep an eye on you. Not to go into the details, but I know what to look for with bipolar disorder. Especially now that I know what's going on."

Wow. Maybe she's bipolar. Or someone in her family. The hesitation in her voice worries me.

"But?" I ask.

"But I won't be able to help you at the restaurant," she says. "That's five hours a week of intense training. In a noisy, fast-moving kitchen. Chaz loves working with our students. But he has to run the back of the house."

My hands start shaking more as I sip my tea. "Please don't tell me I have to drop it."

Mrs. Rosembert refills her mug. "I'm not going to say that. That is for you to decide. But it's going to be a lot of pressure. You're still recovering and getting stable. I can see you're wound pretty tight right now. I'm asking if you really feel ready to handle that. Be honest with yourself."

"I have to be ready," I say. "I need to stay on track."

She sips and studies me. "You're always so passionate about cooking. This illness does not have to stop that. But you must learn how to work with it."

I gulp the rest of the tea and move to the sink to wash my cup. "I'm seeing my therapist. Trying to get enough sleep. Taking my meds, even though they suck."

"Do you want to disclose your illness to Chaz?" she asks. "Let him know what's up so he can be aware?"

That sounds risky. I don't want everyone knowing my business. "What if that backfires? Makes him not want me there?"

"That would be discrimination," she says. "He can't do

that. And he doesn't think like that anyway. It could help him be more understanding if you have any symptoms flare up."

My body won't stand still. I pace around, peeking in the fridge and cabinets at class supplies. Trying to find something that will distract me from my boiling emotions.

"Think about it," she goes on. "Talk to your dad. You'd need to share the details directly with Chaz. Or give me written permission to tell him for you. It's an option. We could do it before your orientation so he has time to come up with ideas."

She starts packing up. "At least the training doesn't start until late October. Promise me you'll keep focusing on your health, okay? The better you're feeling, the better that's going to go."

My insides calm a bit. "I promise."

"I've got a meeting before I can head out to enjoy the last of the heat," she says. "Before the cold creeps in and makes me miserable."

That makes me smile. An old joke between us.

We say goodbye, and I head for home. A text is waiting for me.

Gavin: *How'd it go with Mrs. Rosembert?*

Me: *She's got my back. Like you said*

Gavin: *Good. You're her favorite, after all*

Me: *Hah, hah. She appreciates someone who knows the difference between poaching and braising*

Gavin: *Food nerd*

Ian and Josie don't respond, but they're at their new after-school jobs right now. I'm wiped. Maybe I'll nap a bit before dinner. And then try to make sense of the homework already piling up. I wanted my routine back, and I got it. Now it's time to figure it out.

CHAPTER 6

Mrs. Rosembert tosses out advice as she strolls among the stations.

It's food lab day. We're working on knife skills and stir-fry. I'm in my happy place. It helps that we move around a lot. It feels like ants crawling all over my legs when I'm stuck sitting in other classes.

We're in the third week of school, and I'm hanging in there. Day by day. That's what everyone keeps telling me. Take it day by day. Yada yada. It's one of those sayings that can be easily picked apart.

At home, Dad watches me like a hawk, looking for any signs I can't hack it. I let him go over my homework with me at night. It makes him feel more in control of something out of our control. Truth is, I need the help right now. Not that I'm telling him that.

"Ow!" A thin stream of blood leaks from my finger onto my carrots.

"Cleanup on aisle nine!" Mrs. Rosembert calls.

Students chuckle. This is her way of announcing when someone cuts or burns themselves. But only when it's a small injury. She's serious and moves fast if it's a big deal.

"Slow down and stay out of your head, Kai," she says, passing me a Band-Aid. "And please don't put those in your dish."

She winks and strolls on to inspect another student's progress.

After cooking class, I gulp down a bunch of water and refill my bottle. I'm ridiculously thirsty all the time because of the meds. A million ideas about how I can launch my food career bounce around my mind as I head to Krissie's office for my lunchtime pill.

"Well?" That's her way of asking if I'm in a good place or not.

"Maybe a two on the edginess scale," I report.

"Wow! That's a big change from yesterday," she says while she retrieves my medicine. "Any ideas on why?"

I nod to another kid as he comes in. He's here around the same time every day for his insulin. He nods back. That's better than the cold shoulder I still get from most.

"Cooking always puts me in a good mood. Even when I get injured." I show her my cut finger.

She grins. "Ah, you got a boo-boo. Want a SpongeBob Band-Aid?"

I laugh and take my pill. Krissie's easy to talk to. I decide to float one of my ideas by her. "I'm thinking of starting a food truck."

"Now? Or you mean later, after you finish your training and you're an old man in his twenties?"

I'm not sure. I do circles around her office while telling her and the other kid all about the food truck. I can't remember the other kid's name. I could ask, but that feels awkward. I'll ask Krissie another time when he's not there. And if he's friendly and has the right skills, I'll let him in on my food truck venture.

Krissie waves her hands for me to stop.

"Man, you are high on the energy level today," she says. "The food truck idea sounds amazing. For your *future*. Keep it on the back burner. For now, you better head to lunch before you run out of time."

I wave goodbye and head out to find my friends. But they've already eaten and left for class by the time I get to our spot. I wanted to lay out the food truck details to them. They'd be all in.

"No they wouldn't," the man says. "They'd just pretend to help. They're pretenders."

I try to ignore him.

Some kids I sort of know are still eating. I could sit alone to eat. But maybe it's time to test the waters, see if I'm still an outcast.

"How's everybody doing?" I say as I sit at their table. I unwrap my turkey and Havarti panini.

"Hi, Kai," one girl replies. Mary, I think.

I get an uncomfortable "hi" from the other girl and boy.

"I've spaced on your names. Sorry," I tell them.

"Abby," the girl answers. She starts packing up her lunch.

"Baker," the boy says.

"Baker! Love it." I laugh. "Are you doing culinary arts? You should. With a specialty in baking. Then you could open your own Bakery by Baker business. Or maybe Baker's Bakery."

They smile while getting up from the table.

"Gotta go," Mary says. "See you around."

And that tells me all I need to know. Grippy grabs my insides. But I finish my lunch and try to look like I'm totally fine eating alone.

I head to Earth Science after I finish. It's a long class. Mr. Torez lets me stand in the back if I'm feeling too twitchy. It helps me concentrate. Today's one of those days. At least Gavin's in this class too. This is his thing, what he wants to study in college. That gives me an easy tutoring option if I need it.

"You okay?" he asks as we file out of the classroom. "You seem pretty wired."

"Yep, I'm good. Need to talk to all of you about my food truck idea."

Gavin starts down a different hallway. "I've got geology club now. Remember? Fill us in tomorrow night at Josie's."

I wave him off. I've got an appointment with Hunter anyway. I text Dad about my idea on the way to the bus stop.

The clinic lobby has an odor from too many people who smoke. This gives me an idea. I could try smoked beef in my yakisoba. That's one of my signature dishes. I need to keep experimenting with versions of it.

I watch the other people in the lobby try to hold their act together, just like they're watching me. One guy's given up. He's carrying on a conversation with an invisible group while pacing back and forth. At least this is a safe place to do that. But he can't always be within the clinic walls. Does he talk inside his head outside the clinic? When he's with people who don't know how to react to his behavior?

I tell the receptionist I'll wait outside.

Eventually, Hunter pops his head out the door.

"Inside or outside today?" he asks. "Nice afternoon for a walk."

"Walk," I say. I start toward the river trail that runs behind the office building. "I'm going to open a food truck," I tell Hunter after he catches up.

"Interesting. With an Asian-Pacific Islander menu or what?" he asks.

"Of course. But not your standard stuff. Unique dishes."

We walk along the river. I like to go fast. Hunter matches my speed. He doesn't look much older than me. But I guess he's in his late twenties. He asks the usual questions therapists like to ask. I give the usual answers.

I grab a protein bar and my water bottle from my backpack. After I snarf down the bar and gulp the water, I complain about being so hungry and thirsty all the time. Hunter promises to let my psychiatrist, Dr. Chu, know.

When he asks if I'm hearing the voices, I decide to be honest.

"One. The man. Not sure where the others went. On vacation?"

That makes Hunter laugh. "Well, they're missing our best weather, if that's the case. Do they have names?"

"No. Should they?" I ask.

He shakes his head. "Just a question. And it's early days. Maybe they'll stick around, maybe they're passing through."

"Well, I don't want to give them names. And I don't want them sticking around."

We reach our turning-around point and head back toward the clinic.

"How's it feeling with school now?" Hunter asks.

I tell him the truth again, even though he can't do anything about it. "I'm mostly being avoided. Or watched. Everyone is waiting to see if I flip out again. Like today. My friends weren't around, so I tried eating lunch with some other kids. They left almost as soon as I sat down."

We're both working up a sweat. Hunter waves me over to a bench.

"I'm sorry about that, Kai. And at home?" he asks. He sits on the bench, and I pace in front of it.

What do I say about home? That Dad's walking on

eggshells, waiting for me to crack? For our whole family to crack?

Finally, I say, "I feel bad for my dad. This stuff is killing him."

"He seems like a good guy," Hunter says. "It takes time to adjust to things when an illness like this happens in a family. We can talk about it more next week when you both come in."

"Did he tell you about my mom being bipolar?" I ask.

Hunter hesitates. "I saw that mentioned in your hospital notes."

Nice. Everyone knew except me.

He jumps up to follow when I continue walking to the clinic. "What do you think about that?" he asks.

I don't know how to explain my feelings. So many thoughts and questions race through my mind.

"Not sure," I say. "It's been weird for years because she doesn't talk to me, only Dad. I haven't spent much time thinking about her. Now I can't get her off my mind."

"Do you want to talk to her now?" he asks.

"My family thinks it could help me," I explain. "But that feels like weird on top of weird. How do you go from no relationship to suddenly having a cozy mother-son bonding moment just because we both have this?"

We hover by the clinic entrance. "Well, I don't know the details about her circumstances," Hunter says. "And your questions are understandable. We can keep exploring them together if you want."

We finish up, and I check my phone on the bus home. Dad texted a quick thumbs-up about my food truck idea. He manages production at a nearby fruit packing plant. He's always on the road to farms, vineyards, and restaurants in the area. He can help me with research. I text back that I had a good appointment with Hunter. Maybe that will help him stop worrying so much. I don't share about the conversation about my mom. Best to let that marinate for now.

At least my friends and I are finally getting together

tomorrow. I'll run the food truck idea by them then. I've missed our Friday night hangouts, just chilling and joking around.

Friend therapy. Dr. Chu and Hunter would approve.

CHAPTER 7

My friends are already laughing when I arrive. I guess they started the party without me. My hands are full, so I thump on Josie's door with my foot. They don't hear me. I rest my bags on the porch and knock harder.

Josie swings open the door. Finally.

"Yes! I was hoping you'd make us something," she says, eyeing my food supplies.

I push a bag her way to carry.

Ian and Gavin make space so we can squeeze into the kitchen. Sub sandwiches and chips crowd the counter.

"We know, we know," Josie says. "Boring stuff. But we've got you to amp it up."

"Suck-ups," the man says. "Sure you want to be here?"

Shut up, I hiss at him.

My friends go quiet. Crap. I said that out loud.

"What's up?" Gavin asks.

They all look concerned.

"Sorry. My bad," I say, trying to shrug it off. "I was thinking of something in my head."

I need this night. I can do this. I take a deep breath and try to relax.

"Okay, I'm testing a new concept on you tonight." I pull out my board and food tubs. "Forget your standard charcuterie boards with the same old cheeses, meats, crackers, and other things. I'm fusing together Asian and Pacific Northwest flavors."

"I'm in," Ian says. "Let's eat."

They help me arrange the small bites on my board. Salmon poke. Rice cubes crusted with sesame seeds. Pear jam. Rice crackers. Blackberries.

"You are the master chef!" Josie says.

"This looks so tasty," Gavin adds.

Josie's parents are at a movie. So we take everything to the living room and spread out. Our conversation jumps from one topic to the next.

Ian tells funny stories about his after-school job at a

taqueria. Josie complains about her boss at the bookstore. Gavin is getting up early tomorrow for a field trip to study protected fossils.

"Earth to Kai," Josie says, tossing a rice cube at me.

"What?" I pack the rice even tighter before throwing it back. It smacks her in the face.

"Ow!"

Guess I threw it harder than I meant to. I cringe.

"I was asking how it's going at school," she says. "Don't get upset about it."

They're all staring at me.

"Sorry. I didn't mean to do that," I say. "Just don't startle me."

"Got it. Sorry," she says.

Ian fills my cup with more soda. "What's the latest with you? How's culinary arts?"

I stand and start telling them about my food truck idea. I think better when I'm moving. But Josie's living room isn't very big. I have to squeeze around the furniture and my friends to do my circles.

They're shooting looks at each other.

I stop moving. "What? Why are you making faces?"

They don't say anything. Then Ian comes over to take my temperature.

"You've got a lot of energy to burn," he says. "It's a little hard to follow."

I push away his hand. "So you think it's a bad idea?" I ask.

"Not what I said." Ian holds his hands up. "But I'm a little worried about how you're feeling."

Gavin tugs on Ian's shirt to pull him back to the couch. Then he pats a spot on his other side and signals for me to sit down. I shake off my irritation and plop next to him.

"New subject. I had to do my first highway trip in driver's ed the other day. Yikes," Gavin says.

"That's me next week," Josie says. "This week it was parallel parking. At least I didn't scratch the other cars."

Ian pulls up a website with used cars for sale. "This is why I'm washing dishes and bussing tables. Eyes on the prize."

"Are you doing driver's ed this semester, Lummy?" Josie asks me.

I laugh. "Right. That's on pause for me. I have to be super stable before Dad will even talk about it."

The conversation stalls. The man fills my head with insults about my friends.

"Winter dance," Ian tosses into the awkward silence. "Go? Ignore?"

They debate back and forth. They talk about whether they'll be brave and ask someone. What they'd wear.

What does it matter? My muddled brain gets a flash of clarity. Things are shifting in our group. And I'm being left behind.

It's too hot in here. I grab my board and head to the kitchen.

"What's up, Kai?" Ian asks.

"I'm fine. I just need some fresh air," I say. "Think I'll take off."

Gavin joins me. "I have to be up at six for the field trip. Probably best for me to call it an early night too."

He helps me pack up.

"Love the charcuterie fusion idea," he says as we grab our things and head to the door. "You could expand that to other regions or cultures."

At least he gets it.

"I'll include them on the menu when I take my food truck to wineries," I explain.

Josie and Ian join us at the door.

"Text when you get home?" Josie asks.

"Why?" I ask.

Ian sighs. "Just text, Lummy."

Crap. Maybe I blew it tonight. This wasn't like the fun nights we used to have.

"Maybe they're not the great friends you thought they were," the man says.

Gavin walks with me a few blocks until he needs to turn off.

"We're here for you," he says as we part. "Best friends, right?"

I hope so. I don't want my friendships to change.

Not when everything else in my life is so different now.

Hopefully this was a one-off. Next Friday will be better. It has to be.

CHAPTER 8

My phone has a few new messages when I wake up at noon on Saturday.

Ian: *You okay, Kai? Still up waiting to hear from you*

Josie: *And thanks for the charcuterie. Tasty*

Gavin: *It's an hour when no one should be awake. I'm off on my trip. Probably no bars until I get back tonight*

Josie: *Have fun*

Ian: *Hope you catch lots of action. With fossils, I mean*

Josie: *You up yet, Kai?*

Ian: *Need to hear from you, Lummy, or I'm heading over this afternoon*

I was up for hours after getting home from Josie's. Couldn't sleep. Didn't want to, anyway. I type out a quick reply to our group chat.

Me: *I'm up. Forgot to text last night. Sorry*

Josie: *Glad you're okay. I'm doing history homework today. You?*

Ian: *Stay connected please*

Me: *Yeah. Sorry if I was a little off last night*

Josie: *We're good. Tap me for history if you need*

When I stand up, my feet crunch on sheets of notebook paper tossed on the floor. Scrawled menu ideas. Space layout sketches. A list of business names.

My brain was busy last night. Now my body is paying for it. It feels like I'm underwater, weighed down with stones. My brain has crashed too.

I find Dad in the garden. He's pruning back plants that won't grow through the upcoming cold months.

"You gonna change?" he asks. I look down and realize I'm still in yesterday's clothes.

He hands me a sprig of rosemary. Its earthy fragrance wakes up my brain a bit. It's a winter survivor.

"Can we run by a few wineries this weekend?" I ask.

"When and why?" he asks.

I follow him as he moves to a new section of plants. "I need to research my food truck idea."

He tries to hide it, but I can see the worry.

"How about today you clean up and focus on your homework?" he says. "Lonny and Serena are coming over later. You can help me cook for them. Then tomorrow afternoon, we can run by some wineries."

At least it wasn't a no.

The weekend turns into a thick fog.

Me reading the same textbook sentences over and over while nothing sinks in.

Dad finishing the cooking after I burn the chicken. Me shoveling in the mediocre food anyway, trying to satisfy the gnawing hunger that never leaves.

Lonny and Serena cushioning me between them on the couch, not talking but somehow saying a lot.

Sleep taking me deep. So deep that Dad has to shake me awake.

We miss going to the wineries.

And Monday morning, I miss my first classes too. Dad

and I are at the clinic for an appointment the hospital scheduled back when I was discharged.

Hunter is there. And Dr. Chu. He's nice enough. He looks and acts like what you'd expect from a psychiatrist.

Hunter's already shared how I'm doing with Dr. Chu. They ask me how I think the treatment is going. Then they want to hear what Dad thinks. I brought my notebook, so I work on my food truck idea while he talks. It's hard to control the shaking in my hands. My handwriting looks like it's from a kindergartener practicing their first words.

"Do you feel that way, Kai?" Dr. Chu asks, breaking into my thoughts.

"What?" I ask.

"Are you feeling really hyper some days and really low-energy other days?"

"Guess so." I shrug. That doesn't really describe the roller coaster ride my brain and body are on. "It's the meds. They suck. Can I stop them yet?"

"The meds are important for keeping you well, Kai," Dr. Chu says. "Tell me what's going on."

Dad jumps in. "He can't eat enough. He's always hungry. And thirsty. He's always been thin, but he's gaining weight. And he looks so zoned out."

"The meds make me dizzy," I add. I hold up my hands. "And I'm sick of this shaking."

Dr. Chu goes through the list of meds. He talks about switching one of them for a med that doesn't make people so hungry and thirsty.

"With bipolar disorder, we want the meds to keep your mood stable. And to control symptoms like mania and hallucinations," he explains. "But we may need to try some different ones over the next several months. Or change the dosages. We'll learn what works best for you."

"Months? I have to take these for months?" I cry.

Dad squeezes my arm. "Your mom still takes her meds, many years later. It's important to stay healthy."

I shoot Hunter a look at the mention of my mom.

"Bipolar disorder can play out differently for different people. So what works for your mom may be different from what works for you," Hunter says. "But it is a chronic condition. It doesn't go away. We'll keep working on how you manage symptoms. Meds are only one part of the formula."

Dr. Chu types fast on his computer. He explains the new med to Dad. He says I'll slowly go off the old one before starting the new one.

"It's still early days, Kai," he says. "Based on what I'm hearing and seeing, you aren't out of the woods yet."

My body goes on high alert. "Are you saying I need to go back to the hospital?"

He quickly waves his hands. "No. But recovery takes time. And we don't know your new baseline yet."

"Baseline?" I ask. That word keeps coming up.

"Your new normal," Hunter explains. "For example, we'll want to get a handle on what's a normal range of moods for you."

"I still recommend you enroll in the early intervention program," Dr. Chu says. "I know you're worried about it affecting your school schedule. But it would be a short-term investment of time to get to your goals. It would reduce the chance of you missing more school or even a job opportunity later. And it would reduce the chance of you needing to be treated in the hospital again."

Hunter leans forward. "We're learning how important it is to act after people experience a first episode of psychosis. What we do now can make a big difference as you become a young adult."

I can't sit still any longer. I get up and pace around the cluttered office. "I heard it's a lot of group therapy. I had enough of that in the hospital. That was the worst."

"It's different in an outpatient setting," Hunter says. "People are more stable and working on staying that way. And the program isn't all group work. You'd have one-on-one time with the clinical team. There are also activities for your family so they can understand what's happening. It gives them support so they can support you."

Dad pulls in his legs when I loop past him. "I've been reading up on it. This program sounds like a good thing, Kai. We don't want to go backward, eh?"

His shaking voice makes me stop. I know he's scared.

"But I don't need this, Dad," I say. I need him to believe me. "Stop bringing it up."

"I want you to be safe. And feel good," he says.

I can't handle the tears brimming in his eyes.

"Are we done? Can we go?" I ask Hunter and Dr. Chu.

"Yes, we're done for now," Dr. Chu says. "But do you remember which medicine is the most important for you?"

My hand is on the doorknob, but I wait for his answer.

"Sleep," he says. "Sleeping well, resting, and avoiding stressful situations. These can help prevent symptoms from being triggered. Okay?"

I nod and head out before they can keep pressuring me into adding more chaos to my life.

Dad's quiet all the way to school. I feel bad, but my mind is turning a million cartwheels. I decide to make Dad something special when I get home tonight.

We eat dinner while streaming an episode of *The Great Food Truck Race* so I can take notes. Then I bring out the mango mousse I made as a surprise.

"Ta-da!" I say.

Good. That got a smile.

"It's going to be okay, Dad," I say. "Trust me."

He pulls me into a hug and heads to the kitchen to clean up.

Later, after attempting to figure out my Earth Science homework, I call Gavin for help. After we're done, I head to the kitchen to give in to the hunger. Maybe I'll give it a name. That'll make Hunter laugh.

I can hear Dad on the phone in his room. It only takes a second for me to realize he's talking about me. I pause to listen.

"I just want to do it differently this time," he says. "I knew nothing about bipolar disorder back then. I didn't do much to help her."

He listens to the other person. It has to be my auntie or uncle.

"This program sounds like his best shot at getting better. But he keeps saying no." He pauses.

There's a man's voice on the other end. Uncle Lonny.

"I could do that," Dad answers. "It'll make me the most unpopular dad in the world. But I don't think he gets how serious this is."

Crap. He's going to force me to do that program. Grippy is like an anchor in my chest. What am I going to do?

"Told you not to trust anyone," the man says.

Dad and Lonny talk about my meds and how they think I'm still manic. When it's clear they're wrapping up, I walk to the kitchen.

Dad doesn't come out. I'm glad. I don't think I could pretend things are okay when he's determined to mess up my life.

They accuse me of being manic because I'm excited about my ideas and busy making plans. Why is that a bad thing? I look up the word. Overexcited. Hyper. Agitated. Frantic. Feverish.

Hah!

Me: *Hey, Dr. Ian. Just learned that manic can mean feverish. You're on to something!*

Ian: *Why? You feverish now?*

Me: *High on life, my friend*

Ian: *Okay, but try bringing it down a couple of notches if you can*

Me: *Why?*

Ian: *So people don't think you're too hyper*

"He's on their side," the man warns. "Careful."

Sounds like someone got to Ian. Dr. Chu? Hunter? Or maybe my dad.

I don't text back.

CHAPTER 9

I zip my jacket and adjust my backpack. Gavin gets his gear in place. His mom waves goodbye. She'll pick us up after we finish the canyon trail.

"I can't wait to get my license," Gavin says. "Then it's freedom, my friend. Freedom."

Doesn't look like that's in the cards for me. Not after what I overheard Dad say on the phone earlier this week. "I'll be walking and busing until I'm dead and gone," I say. "No driving in my future."

He starts on the trail winding along the burbling river. "No way. And I'm going to give you rides, obviously."

I look at the red rocks where we're headed. "I hope I can make it to the top. I'm not in the best shape."

Gavin glances back. He doesn't mention how rough I look, but it's in his eyes. "Want to go first and set the pace?"

I wave for him to keep going. "You lead. I'll let you know when I need to break or slow down."

I considered backing out this morning. It wasn't a horrible week, even though I barely saw my friends. I survived my classes. Scraped by on homework, thanks to Dad's help. But then Josie and Ian didn't come last night to our normal Friday hangout. Gavin and I had to scrap our plans. I wanted to give our Friday hangout another chance. See if Ian was really turning sketchy. Show them I'm the same Kai as before.

Anger surges through me again. It kept me up most of the night. Along with the man. He reminded me over and over that they've been pretending to be my friends. He's smart about these things.

"What about Gavin?" I kept asking him.

"Good guy," the man said. "But still watch your back. They can turn on you any time."

I almost run into Gavin now. He's standing in the sagebrush, examining some rocks near the trail. I gulp water and grab my beef jerky while I rest against a boulder.

"Ian and Josie suck. Why would they bail like that?" I ask.

Gavin makes notes in his little field journal. "It's best to let it go, Kai," he says. "It was one night."

"Yeah, but they barely texted all week too."

Gavin puts the journal away. "I think they needed a little break after you went off on them at lunch the other day," he says.

What is he talking about? "No way. They weren't around for lunch."

Gavin tugs my sleeve to start back up the trail.

"Yes, on Tuesday," he says. His voice is patient, but I can sense his concern. "You got mad at one of Ian's jokes. You thought he was making fun of you. Josie tried to explain he wasn't. Then you got mad at her too."

My mind races through the week and finally lands on a fuzzy memory of that lunch. I stayed home sick the next day when Dad couldn't get me to wake up.

"So they're avoiding me," I huff as I try to catch my breath.

Gavin slows his pace. "I think they're giving you space."

We hike without talking for a while. That's good because my head is full of talking. The man's telling me *I told you so*. I'm trying to remember how Ian insulted me and how Josie defended him. But food truck ideas are running through my head too.

We make it to a flat resting spot. Good for fueling up. The sun warms my face while the frosty wind tugs my clothes. We watch a hawk circle and soar nearby.

"I think they're having second thoughts about me because of how the other kids act," I say after a few minutes. "Like Dad and my uncle. And probably my aunt. They're going to bring up that special program any day now. I guess everyone's turning against me. He warned me this would happen."

Gavin throws me one of his energy bars. "I really don't think so. And who warned you?"

"Careful," the man whispers.

"No one you know," I say.

Gavin studies me. "It seems like your mind's all over the

place. Any chance trying to keep up at school is triggering symptoms?"

I don't want to talk about this stuff with him.

"Just don't ghost me," I say instead.

"Not happening," he promises.

Even though my body feels weighed down by rocks, we push on to reach the top of the trail.

As we hike, Gavin admits that he's crushing on a girl in his geology club. Great. He'll start spending time with her and ghost me after all.

Then I admit to being nervous about my job training at the bistro. The wait for it to start in late October is killing me. What if they don't like me there? Or I can't keep up?

By the time we make it to the trail's end, I've realized why so many things are out of my control lately. And how to fix it.

I follow Gavin around while he collects dirt and rock samples in small bags. I'm excited about my insight. I try to keep quiet, but it finally spills out of me.

"It's the meds," I explain. "They're messing up my mind. They make me feel worse."

"You said your doctor was switching things up to help," he says, glancing up at me. He rests the samples on a boulder and starts to label them.

"I need to stop the meds," I say, watching him. "That will get me back on track."

Gavin stops his work and grabs my arms. Not hard, but serious.

"No way," he says. "Listen to me good. Do you want to end up back in the hospital?"

"Not going to happen," I say. He doesn't get it. I should have kept my mouth shut.

"Promise me you'll stay on your meds," he pleads. "I'm leaning on the friend pledge."

Great. The friend pledge is the pact the four of us made after we first became friends. Break a promise to the group and you have to eat something gross.

"Are you making a pledge not to ghost me?" I challenge him.

He doesn't hesitate. "Yep. So keep working with your doctor to find the right meds, okay?"

It's not what I want to do. But maybe he really cares. Either way, I can't have him tipping off my dad.

"Fine," I agree. "I'll try to stay on them longer."

Gavin finishes his sample collection a few minutes later. We find a good spot to take in the view. It seems flatter when you're standing at ground level. From up here, it's a rolling patchwork quilt of green farmland mixed with shades of brown grassland and rocky terrain. This is a good reminder. Different perspectives give more clarity about a situation.

We make our way back down the mountain. Gavin calls his mom to pick us up. A million ideas keep bouncing around in my head.

The hike wiped me out. I let Dad make dinner. He nudges me awake on the couch at the end of a movie we were watching.

"Time for meds," he says. "And maybe an early night for you?"

He gets my pills from the lockbox. I go to the kitchen for a glass of water. I count the rainbow of colors and shapes in my palm. And while Dad's still in the living room, I bury the meds I think are giving me trouble at the bottom of the trash.

CHAPTER 10

A worksheet. Mrs. Rosembert has us doing a kitchen math worksheet. And it's kicking my butt.

I try filling in the right numbers on the measuring cup illustration. How many tablespoons and how many ounces for each cup line.

But my brain won't shut up so I can focus. A million thoughts spin together like ingredients blending into a pastry batter. Thoughts about Josie and Ian, my food truck, my meds, my dad, the whispers and fear creeping through my body that I can't explain. Grippy's working overtime.

I skip to the next section. We're supposed to circle which food item in each row weighs more. Oil versus water. Flour versus sugar. And so on.

"This is so easy," a girl says.

I look around. Two classmates nearby have their heads down, working on the assignment. They didn't say anything.

Mrs. Rosembert hovers over my shoulder.

"Grasshopper," she says quietly. "What gives?"

Crap. I can't have her doubting me.

"Nothing," I say quickly. "It's just taking a minute to get my head into it."

I know this is important. But I'd rather be cooking. At least we'll handle ingredients during the second part of class. More kitchen math work, but with measuring and experimenting.

Mrs. Rosembert calls me over when class ends. She's holding my worksheet.

"I know that you know this stuff," she says. "How are you feeling?"

"I'm fine," I lie. I want to trust her, but I don't know if I can.

Her face says she isn't buying it. She studies me over the worksheet. "You look pretty . . . distracted. Maybe this isn't a good day to meet Chaz."

I'm supposed to visit the bistro after school to get oriented before I finally start in a couple of weeks. The thought of not meeting Chaz today sends a bolt of panic through me.

"Why? I said I'm fine." I shift on my feet.

"Why?" she repeats. "Because I see clues that you're not fine. Your tremors have picked up. There's clearly a lot going on in your head. You keep looking at everyone like they're going to attack you. And it seems you haven't changed clothes in a couple of days."

I can't believe she's talking to me like this. "I thought you were on my side!"

She sighs heavily. "I am. That's why I'm being honest. I'm worried you're going to make Chaz concerned about having you there. It's your right to not disclose what's going on. But that means he hasn't planned any adjustments. He's a supportive guy. But he also has a restaurant to run."

Self-control. She needs to see that I can control the jumpiness messing with my insides.

Deep breaths.

Imagine feeling calm.

Silence the noise.

"I am feeling shaky," I finally admit. "But I can do this. I'll run home and change before going over. And I will show him that I'm ready. Please, Mrs. Rosembert."

Her look says I've won. At least for now. "Drop by or send me a note tomorrow about how it went."

I want to kiss her cheek, but that would be weird. I give her a huge smile and a thumbs-up instead, which looks silly. But I've got to show my thanks somehow.

After the fastest shower and change I've ever done, I dash to the bistro with a few minutes to spare. I repeat my strategy before going in.

Deep breaths.

Imagine feeling calm.

Silence the noise.

The loud chatter among the diners and staff jars my brain when I finally go inside. The background jazz music adds another layer of noise. Dishes clank, and servers greet their tables in friendly voices.

Easy does it, I tell myself. It's simply people enjoying a meal. Food I could help prepare if I do this right.

I study the menu while waiting for Chaz. Fresh market salads. Pastas. Soups and chowders. Wood-fired pizzas. Grilled and roasted meats and poultry. Vegetarian and vegan choices too.

"Hey, Kai. Nice to meet you," Chaz says, walking up to me. He shakes my hand.

He looks like a restaurant manager. Confident. In charge. Comfortable with people. All the things I'm not.

I hide my tremoring hands in my pockets.

"Glad to see you studying the menu," he says. "Let's go talk for a few minutes. Then I'll have you observe in the kitchen for a while. We're moving into the busy dinner hour, as you can see."

We squeeze into his small office by the kitchen to talk about my after-school schedule. The kitchen's louder than the front of the house. I try to not jump at every banging pot. I need to tune out the noise and focus on what Chaz is saying.

I'll be starting on the food prep stations. We head to the kitchen to observe one of them. I immediately see why Mrs. Rosembert hammers at us about knife skills, kitchen math, and technique, technique, technique. The chefs at that station are skilled and precise. I watch them, my stomach flipping nervously.

"You feeling okay?" Chaz asks.

Oh no. I can't blow this. "Fine. Just getting used to the noise."

"That's part of restaurant life. Think you can handle it?" he asks.

"Absolutely."

Chaz sizes me up. I push my hands deeper into my pockets and beg my legs to stop twitching.

"What's your specialty?" he asks.

"Uh, do I need one?" I ask.

"No," he answers. "But if you have a certain skill or type of dish you're interested in working on, we'll make sure you get some practice. If it's within our style and offerings, of course."

That's good. "I've been working on fusing Asian, Pacific

Island, and Pacific Northwest ingredients. But I need to build my skills with vegetarian and vegan dishes."

"Okay," he says. "That lets me know who to pair you with down the road."

Chaz steers me to a stool in the corner where I can sit and watch. He yells out who I am to the kitchen staff, then leaves the room. They nod my way. Some smile. Others don't.

"Watch that guy," the man says as I study the lead chef. "He's ready to give you trouble."

"He can see you're a loser," the girl adds.

"You don't know that," I say. "He's busy cooking."

Crap. Did I say that out loud? No one seemed to notice. They're too busy getting dishes out the door.

A friendly sous chef slips me a plate of fresh pasta in a lemon cream sauce before I leave. My stomach growls. It smells delicious.

An hour later, I'm back home.

"Well?" Dad asks. "How did it go?"

All the nervous energy I've been holding in since arriving at the bistro explodes out of me. "Awesome! I want this so bad for my career."

Dad tosses a bunch of questions at me. *What did Chaz say? What will I be doing? How did I handle the noise? Did I see how fast the kitchen has to work?*

I walk in circles around the house, trying to organize my thoughts. Dad's worked in the food industry for years. He's met Chaz. He knows this restaurant. I share the details.

"It looks like you cleaned up before you went there," Dad says. "That's good."

"Mrs. Rosembert told me to," I say.

"I'm glad you listened to her," he says. "You ignore me when I ask you to do the same thing."

"She was worried," I explain.

That slipped out.

"Really? What did she say?" he asks.

Backtrack, I warn myself.

"The usual worries about her students making a good impression," I say, shrugging.

I can see Dad has something he wants to say. I start heading for my room, not sure I want to hear it.

"I need to fill in my friends about how it went," I tell him.

"Sit with me first," he insists. He pats the open spot next to him on the couch.

I hesitate before plopping down. I pull out my phone to text Gavin. Should I bother including Josie and Ian?

"Restaurants can be very stressful," Dad says. "Hunter and Dr. Chu keep bringing up how stress can trigger symptoms. More psychosis."

I'll include Josie and Ian. Seems like they're avoiding me at school. It's a good test to see if they're really ghosting me.

"The school stress seems hard enough to manage," he continues. "I'm worried this will be too much to handle."

I pause in typing my message and look up at him.

"It doesn't feel stressful when I'm cooking," I say.

"I think we have to accept that this diagnosis isn't going away," he says. "Last spring, I didn't know what was happening. But now I recognize the signs."

My heart races. Maybe me ditching certain meds isn't working fast enough. Is he going to take me back to the hospital?

"I did fine at the restaurant. Chaz liked me."

"That's good. I bet he'd be fine with you postponing the training until you feel better," Dad says.

"No way!" I jump up. "I'm doing this now. We agreed. You can't suddenly change your mind. Stop trying to control me!"

I rush out of the room before he can say anything more. I barricade myself in my room and text my friends. About the bistro. About Dad trying to ruin things. About my latest food truck menu.

Only Gavin replies. There's the answer to my test. How disappointing.

Later, Dad knocks on my door. "Med time."

Tonight, he hangs out nearby. I've been trashing the meds when I can. But I can't get away with it tonight. A guy I met in the hospital showed me how he hid the pills deep in his cheeks and pretended to swallow. It worked until the staff got wise and started checking his mouth. But Dad's not that smart.

Time for me to cheek the meds. It's the only way for me to take back my life.

CHAPTER 11

I'm standing in my usual spot at the back of World Lit, trying to concentrate.

"Shhhhh," I whisper. "I can't hear."

Two kids sitting in the back glance at me and then around me. They can't see the man. Or the girl. I don't see them either. But they sound real. I think they're real. But they're talking up a storm, and I can't hear Mr. Cooper.

The counter I'm leaning against is a mess of books, papers, and maps. I try to stay quiet while I straighten things up.

"Thanks for organizing my piles," Mr. Cooper says. He's at my side and helps me finish.

I look back to see that class is over. But Gavin is there. He isn't in this class. And he looks like someone died.

"Hey, Gav," I say. "What's with the serious face?"

"Can I walk with you to Krissie's office?" he asks.

I forgot that's next. I want to skip it. She's helping them put more poison in my body.

"Nah. I'll catch you later," I say.

Mr. Cooper squeezes my shoulder. "I think it would be a good idea for you to go with Gavin. I love seeing good friends helping each other. I'll see you later, Kai."

I'm not sure how Gavin is helping me. But we head toward the nurse's office.

"I'm still thinking about that barbeque place we found this weekend," he says. "We'll definitely have to go back."

"Barbeque?" I didn't even see Gavin over the weekend. "You're messing with me. I haven't seen you for at least a week."

He pats my back. "Okay, maybe I'm getting my days confused."

Krissie's waiting in her doorway. Gavin watches me go in. He still looks like someone died.

I tidy up her supplies while she gets my med. She hands the pill to me and doesn't turn away. I swallow the poison. Hope she's happy.

"How's your sleep?" she asks.

"Not getting much. Don't need much. Lots to do."

She grabs an orange juice for me. "What's taking up so much time that you don't need to sleep?"

"I've got to perfect my food truck plan," I explain. "Lots of trucks fail after a year because the owners didn't really think through their plan. I've got to be extra smart about this."

She takes the empty bottle from me and tosses it. Did I drink that already?

"Yes, Mrs. Rosembert mentioned how focused you are on your food truck. Sounds like it's going to be amazing."

Wait a minute. Why would my nurse and my culinary teacher be talking? Then it dawns on me. I should have seen this coming.

"You're going to steal my idea! I trusted you two. You said you had my back. So you could stab it, I guess."

"Keep your voice down, Kai," she says.

Two other students are waiting for her in the doorway. They're staring at me with wide eyes.

"This is none of your business," I tell them.

Krissie studies me. "Stay here so we can talk, okay?" She steps away to go help the two waiting students.

"Told you she was a pretender," the man says. The girl laughs and laughs.

I make circles around Krissie's office. It helps to keep moving.

"Let's go," the man says. The girl agrees.

"No, I need to hear her admit she's stealing my idea," I tell them.

When Krissie comes back, I whirl to face her. "How could you betray me like this?"

She sits and waves for me to sit too. No way. I stand against the counter.

"Kai, I'm worried your brain is misfiring," she says.

"Well, if that's true, it's the poison pills you force me to take."

"Your thoughts are all over the place." She shakes her head. "You sound paranoid. You look like a truck ran over you. Are the voices louder now?"

"Let's get out of here," the girl says. "She's going to call the hospital."

We take off before Krissie can do anything else to us. I ignore her calling my name as I go.

People are starting to pack up from lunch. Maybe I'll skip culinary arts. I can't face my traitor teacher.

Gavin appears out of nowhere. He's with a student I don't recognize.

"You know Quinn, right?" Gavin asks me.

Quinn hangs back, giving me space. That's good. I hate it when someone acts fake nice and gets too close when they're just meeting you.

"He's the student mental health first aid coordinator," Gavin says.

Why is he wasting my time with this? I need to figure out my next move.

Quinn hands me a water bottle. "I've been in your shoes, Kai. Gavin thought you might want to talk with someone who understands."

"Understands what?" I ask.

"Your illness," Gavin says. "It looks like you're having symptoms."

What is with everybody today? I ignore his comment and instead twist the water bottle open. I'm thirstier than I realized. But then I gag on the water. I can't let my guard down.

"What did you put in this?" I ask Quinn. "Are you trying to knock me out? Or get rid of me?"

"It's only water," he says. "Do you want to take a walk? Talk and burn some energy?"

Gavin nudges me to follow them. I head the opposite direction.

The bell rings. Students swarm the hallway like angry hornets.

Well, well. There's Ian and Josie. They look so cozy. Not a care in the world.

"Hey, traitors," I call to them. "Remember me? The best friend you've abandoned?"

They glance at each other. They know they've been caught.

"Hey, Lummy," Ian says, walking over. "I've been texting you. But you don't reply."

"Well, that's a lie," I say.

"Me too," Josie says.

"Another lie." I cross my arms.

Some kids are staring. They're probably glad to see Ian and Josie getting called out.

"Where's your phone?" Ian asks.

I don't actually know where it is. Haven't seen it for days.

"It looks like you're not feeling great," he says. "Do you want me to walk home with you? Or I can call your dad to pick you up."

"He deserves an Oscar for playing the concerned friend role," the girl says.

The man laughs. "That's a good one."

"I just wanted to get on track with our Friday nights," I say to Ian and Josie. "But you two ditched me."

I look around at the crowd watching me expose them. "Who's taking my place? Watch your back with these two."

Mr. Brown parts the crowd. "Hey, Kai. Let's take the volume down."

"You tell *them* to take it down," I say. "I keep trying, but they don't listen."

"Who?" he asks, guiding me forward. "I don't hear anyone else yelling."

"The man and the girl. They won't shut up. I have to talk louder to hear over them."

He gestures for me to follow him. After a moment, I do. But first, I give Ian and Josie another death glare. Gavin's standing nearby with that other kid . . . Finn or Quinn, I can't remember. Gavin's staring at the floor and shaking his head. I'm sure we'll talk later about how bad Ian and Josie are treating me.

The crowd parts around us as I walk after Mr. Brown. I can feel their stares.

We make it to his office. "Are they inside or outside your head?" he asks. He sits on the exercise ball at his desk.

I don't know anymore. A tsunami of exhaustion slams my body. I don't even have the energy to shrug.

"Let's get you home so you can rest up," Mr. Brown says. His calm voice is like a lullaby. "Your dad is on his way."

CHAPTER 12

I smell sautéed garlic and ginger. My stomach grumbles. The man and the girl are still yapping away, but the faint sound of sizzling onions breaks through. Other voices murmur words I can't pick out. Terrific. All I need are more voices in my head.

It's dark, and I'm trapped. Am I tied up? Dad must have forced me into the hospital. I push and tug and finally loosen the restraints. Wait, no. It's just bedsheets tangled around me.

I find the light switch. Yes, I'm definitely in my room. At least I think it's my room. It looks like an earthquake hit it. Maybe Dad has been searching through my stuff.

The extra voices seem real. I creep into the hallway. I peer into the kitchen. Lonny and Serena are cooking dinner.

Serena notices me spying on them. "There's our sweet boy. Food soon, yeah?"

Lonny wipes his hands on a kitchen towel and moves my way. He has me in a bear hug before I can escape. The man and the girl start yelling and threatening him.

"We love you so much, Kai," my uncle says. "We'll figure this out."

He finally lets me go.

"Figure what out?" I ask. "Where's Dad?"

"He'll be home soon," Lonny says.

I flee to the living room so there's space between us. I turn on a cooking show. No good. Everything is too loud and foggy. I'm starving. But what if they're planning to trick me? What if they put something in my food?

"You want to shower before we eat?" Serena calls. "The warm water will feel calming."

The front door opens. In comes Dad.

And Gavin. And Hunter.

Why would they be here? Are they real? No, they can't

be. Great, now I have voices coming to life outside my head. What did the doctors call those? Visual hallucinations.

"I know it's a surprise to see me here," Hunter says. He watches me circle the living room.

"You're not real," I say. "I guess I've moved to the next level."

"Nope," he chuckles. "I'm real. Promise."

"And him?" I ask, nodding at Gavin.

"I'm real, Kai," Gavin says. He doesn't chuckle.

"You can poke us if you want," Hunter adds.

I don't want to get too close, but that's a good idea.

They both pass the poke test. They're real. I back away. I'm so confused.

"Why are you here?" I ask. Maybe I promised to cook them something special and forgot it was tonight.

Serena and Lonny smile at me while they set dishes and food on the table.

"Food's ready," Dad says. His voice shakes, and his eyes are bloodred with a million lines of sadness.

"Why have you been crying, Dad?" I ask. "Are you sick? Did something happen?"

I hug him tight.

"Thank you for that," he whispers. When he pulls away, my shirt has a wet stain from his tears. I don't know what to say to make him feel better.

Everybody grabs food and eats standing up or perched on the couch. Serena gives me a plate of shrimp fried rice. It wobbles in my hands. Most of the food tumbles to the floor. I shovel in what's left. I can't remember if I ate earlier today.

"We're all here for you, Kai," Dad says. He hasn't touched his food.

"Why?" I ask with my mouth full.

"Your symptoms are back," Hunter says. "We want to keep you out of a full-blown crisis if possible."

"They've probably called the ambulance already," the man warns.

"Krissie and Mr. Brown filled me in on what happened today," Dad says.

That pisses me off. "Whatever they're saying is a lie. I'm only tired."

Dad keeps blinking fast. It looks like he's trying hard not to cry again. "Gavin was there too. And I've seen this building up. You're heading for a breakdown."

I shoot daggers at my friend. My *former* friend. "You're a traitor!"

Gavin doesn't say anything. He still looks like someone died.

Lonny moves in front of me. Too close. I try to move away. He pulls my forehead against his.

"We are your family," he whispers. "We know when you're soaring. We know when you're low. We will always do everything we can to help you. Hear me, my boy. You are not well."

I am so tired. Tired of the voices. Tired of feeling so wired. Tired of feeling tired. Tired of trying to stay off the edge of this bipolar cliff.

Lonny pulls away, and I sink onto the couch. Hunter takes a seat next to me.

"How many voices?" he asks.

"Only the two. That's good, right?" I ask.

"Are they talking all the time or do they just make appearances?" he asks.

"They're yammering and yapping constantly," I say. "I can't hear the teacher in class. I can't even hear myself think to finish homework."

"Any thoughts of trying to hurt yourself?" Hunter asks. "Or anyone else?"

They asked me that all the time in the hospital. I hated it then. I hate it now. "No! I'm sick of those questions."

Hunter puts up his hands. "I know. But it's important to ask. I hope you'll tell me if the answer is ever yes. Or tell any of us. Or the crisis line."

Now Dad's on my other side. He takes my shaking hands and massages them gently.

"Are the meds always going in?" he asks.

The man and the girl scream to not tell him.

But I'm so tired of lying.

"No" is all I can say.

Dad's body folds, and he starts sobbing. No. I can't handle seeing my dad like this.

Hunter reaches across me and squeezes my dad's arm. "Try to take some breaths, Felix." He turns back to me. "How often are they not going in, Kai? All of the time? Most of the time? Or every now and then?"

I lean against my dad. Maybe that will help him stop crying. "Most," I answer.

Lonny and Serena pull Dad up and take him to the kitchen. I try to hear what they're saying, but the man and the girl have other plans.

"Kai." Hunter nudges my arm. I force my attention to him. "I was saying that it's best for you to stay home from school for a few days."

This can't be happening.

"Will you agree to restarting your meds?" he asks. He watches me seriously.

"The meds that are poisoning me? The meds that make me feel like crap?"

Serena brings me another plate of food and sets it

on the coffee table. She runs her fingers through my hair and kisses my head before heading back to the kitchen.

"Some of this is your brain tricking you," Hunter says. "The meds are not poison. But I agree they are complicated and can have some side effects. We'll keep working with Dr. Chu to figure out the right combo for you. It can take time."

I wolf down more fried rice. "And if I don't take the meds?"

Hunter sighs. "Based on what I'm seeing, I think you'll get sicker and not be able to tell what's real or not."

Too much food too fast makes me gag. Or maybe it's seeing my plans go in the toilet. "*This* is ruining my goals."

"I look at it as hitting the pause button to help *save* your goals. I'd like to turn this around with you," Hunter says.

Everyone's silent. Hours go by. Or maybe it's minutes. I don't know. Lonny and Serena clean up the rice I spilled on the floor.

I don't know what's real or not. They could call an ambulance any time. I guess I'll play their game for now, say what they want me to say. And I'll call Mrs. Rosembert tomorrow while Dad's at work. She'll help me keep my job training on track.

I nod at Hunter.

Dad comes back in and Hunter talks with us about a plan, but I'm not following his words. At least the free time will let me work on my food truck. And if the meds still make me feel worse, that's it. They only get one more chance.

People are leaving. My auntie and uncle give me more hugs and kisses. Hunter promises to call tomorrow. Gavin hovers near the door. I forgot he was here.

"Call me any time," he tells me.

I say nothing back. He's part of their plot to kill my plans and make me fail.

"Fake friend," the man reminds me.

The house feels so quiet once it's just me and Dad again.

"You want to watch a show before bed?" Dad asks. He looks a mess.

I head for my room. "I want to sleep."

He grabs my med box. "Okay. Let's do meds now so I don't have to wake you up in a bit."

He gives me the night pills. I swallow them this time. He stares, so I open my mouth and show that they went down.

We both head to our rooms, too exhausted to say anything more.

CHAPTER 13

It's still dark and cold when I get up to make breakfast. A dream about soft scrambled eggs with cotija cheese pulled me out of bed. I used to like getting up early, doing my thing in the kitchen, surprising Dad with one of my dishes. When did that change?

My mind clicks back to the big intervention. I think that was last week. It's hard to keep time straight.

I kick on the heat and try to be quiet as I make my way to the kitchen. Dad's still sleeping.

My eggs have just set when Dad comes in and starts his coffee.

"Good to see you up and cooking like the old days," he says.

"I was thinking that too."

He disappears to take a shower. I eat my eggs in peace.

No gagging, hooray. And at least I can hold the fork without too much shaking.

I'm deep into a cooking show when Dad joins me on the couch with his coffee and toast. He hands me my morning meds. After I've tossed them in, he waits for me to open my mouth. I don't try to hide how annoying it is as I obey.

"He'll never trust you," the man says.

"Early days, Kai," Dad says. "Early days."

We watch the show without talking. I wish he'd go to work.

Suddenly, I'm pulling myself out of a groggy trance. The sunrise hits me square in the eyes. Guess I crashed on the couch. The TV is off, and Dad is on the phone.

"Yeah, he's starting to leave his room more. That's a good sign," Dad says. Probably talking to Lonny or Serena. Then Dad sees that I'm up. "He's awake now. Let me give him to you."

He hands me his phone.

"Good morning, Kai." It's Hunter. He's called me every

day to check in. I guess I agreed to that the night they all swarmed the house to save me.

"What'd you have for breakfast?" he asks, pulling me out of my head.

"Eggs. Scrambled, with a side of meds," I say. "Very tasty."

He laughs. "How's the gagging?"

"I haven't been doing it as much."

Hunter goes through the rest of his standard questions.

"Do we really need to talk every day?" I ask when I've answered the last one.

"Well, I want to keep a close watch on how it's going with the med change Dr. Chu put in place," he says.

"It seems like you're hoping to hit send on the request to get me committed," I say.

Dad's been listening to our conversation. My comment takes the wind out of his sails.

"Nope, trying to do the opposite," Hunter answers. "Do you have anything else for me, Kai?"

"Nope." I toss the phone back to Dad and head to my room.

I look for clean clothes in a pile on the floor. My hand hits my phone buried at the bottom. It's dead. Takes a while to find my charger and get the phone juicing up. Messages start loading. That surprises me. How long has it been since I checked it? It's like I dropped off the face of the earth.

Gavin: *How are you doing?*

Ian: *I'm sorry this has been rough, Lummy. Still friends? Let me know how to help*

Josie: *Missing you, my friend. Know that we do care about you. We want to help. Just need to know how*

Gavin: *I may swing by later. Okay?*

Gavin: *Thinking about you. Respond when you're ready*

How can I know they really care? Gavin got all in my business and banded together with my family. Now it's like I'm on house arrest. That's the biggest betrayal of all.

I won't answer any of them. They probably want to feed gossipy details to each other.

"Yeah, don't," the man warns. "They'll feed anything you say to your dad and Hunter."

I've also got two voicemails.

The first is from Krissie. She's glad I'm getting help. Call her if I need to talk. She can't wait to see me back. Blah, blah, blah.

The other is from Mrs. Rosembert. It sounds like I called her and asked for her help escaping my dad. There goes her confidence that I can pull this off.

Crap. Mrs. Rosembert's voice jogs my memory.

I rush to find Dad. "I'm supposed to start at the bistro this week!"

He drops the laundry when I startle him.

This is bad. I worked so hard to keep it together so I could do this program. And now I'm blowing it anyway.

"It's okay," Dad says, pulling me into a hug. "Chaz said you can start later. It's okay."

"Chaz won't want me there now," I say. "I hate this!"

I let the pain flow onto his shoulders. Tears I didn't know were building up inside me begin to fall.

"He knows you're sick, but he doesn't know why." Dad speaks in the soft voice he used when I was small. He rocks me back and forth.

"Why is this happening to me?" I cry.

He shushes me and rocks me until my despair drains away. At least for now. Maybe this is just how it's going to be.

Dad finishes folding clothes. He asks if I want to do a *Chopped* challenge with mystery basket ingredients to make our lunch. But I don't have the energy today. He makes us plain grilled cheese sandwiches instead.

"Let's go on a walk," Dad says after I finish another nap.

"Too cold."

"I think fresh air and exercise are as important as your medications," he says.

"Okay, Dr. Felix," I joke. "I'll tell Dr. Chu he has been replaced." But I get up and pull on my shoes.

We bundle up and look at Halloween decorations around our neighborhood. My body feels like it's climbing a mountain, not strolling at a snail's pace on flat ground. Dad realizes he's racing ahead and pulls back.

"Come on, old man," he teases.

"Not sure I'm ready to laugh about it," I say. "This thing is throwing my body forward in time."

Dad takes my arm. "Can you describe what it feels like? What's going on inside?"

We stop to look at an elaborate haunted house in one front yard. We wave when our neighbor glances out the window. He gives us a thumbs-up. Are things good for him? Or does some kind of darkness lurk behind his closed doors? This whole experience has taught me that we don't usually know what's going on with people beyond what we can see.

"Any way to share how it feels?" Dad repeats, bumping his shoulder against mine.

How do I describe this uninvited guest who's moved into my brain and body?

"It's like there's two of me now," I try. "One of them you

know. The other, I don't even know. He just busted in this year. And he's a really confusing guy."

We shuffle on.

"Keep going," Dad says. "I really want to understand it better."

I search for the words. "When he's in control, it's like being in a dream. Sometimes the dream seems real, but I'm pretty sure it isn't. And sometimes I don't know it's a dream until you all tell me later that it wasn't real."

Another neighbor has a candy bowl sitting on a table by the sidewalk, even though it's a few days before Halloween. I choose a peanut butter cup. Dad grabs a tiny bag of jelly beans.

"Okay, so that's when you're having delusions," he says. "How about the mania? What does that feel like?"

I picture that Energizer Bunny in TV commercials. "It doesn't matter if I'm tired. My body wants to keep going. And ideas come at me fast. You know, I don't totally hate it when I feel like that. It's exciting."

Dad's quiet.

"Do you hate it?" I ask.

"It can be scary when you get to several levels past hyper," he admits. "I mean, even your blood pressure was through the roof with this last episode. And it's like you black out. You don't remember big chunks of time."

That explains a lot. And scares me the most.

We turn a corner back onto our street. I'm glad. The cold is creeping into my bones.

"What's the worst thing about your meds?" he asks after a few minutes.

"Foggy brain. Being so tired. Not feeling like myself. How long of a list do you want?" I ask. "At least Dr. Chu took care of me being so thirsty and hungry all the time."

Our house is in sight. This little walk kicked me in the butt.

"Last question," Dad says. "Hallucinations. Can you explain those to me?"

"Do you hear the wind rustling the trees right now?" I ask.

He frowns.

"Sounds real, right?" I prod. "Is it? What if it isn't? How would you know?"

He takes in that reality while we head inside.

The warm air of our house wraps around me like a blanket. My body's exhausted. My mind is quiet for once. The invisible load feels a little lighter. I try not to think about it in case that makes the noise come back. Guess I'm the one walking on eggshells now.

CHAPTER 14

The dice tumble onto the board. Dad taps his little hat along the spaces.

"Pay attention, Kai," Lonny warns. "You're losing out on rent."

Dad lands on one of my properties. "That'll be $26," I announce. I hold out my hand for the fake money Dad owes me.

I watch my dad, Lonny, and Serena like I'm floating above them, not sitting with them at the table for game night. Monopoly this time. A tradition we haven't done for months. We're trying to bring it back now that it's been another week and I'm feeling better.

Am I feeling better? I guess so, in some ways. But a strong sadness has snuck into my body. It's brought new thoughts I can't shake. Now's the time to ask what's been on my mind.

Lonny starts to hand me the dice, but my tremors are worse tonight. He tosses them for me, and I stare at the numbers.

"I was wondering," I say. "Did you ever tell Mom what's been going on with me?"

Dad moves my little penguin along the board and doesn't look at me for a moment. His eyes are cautious when he finally glances up. "I let her know. She was very sorry to hear it."

Serena looks me over. "What's up, my boy?"

"I'm just thinking about her. How she got sick. And now I got sick. How life sucks in that way."

Serena hugs me from the right, while Dad hugs me from the left.

"Your mom had . . . *has* . . . a lot of positive things about her," Lonny says. "Her skill with restoring antiques is incredible. You've inherited her creative talents."

Dad waves his hand around our living room. "You think I'd know how to pick out all of this beautiful furniture? That was your mom."

"Tell me what happened. You've never shared the details," I say. I finally feel ready.

Dad goes to his room and comes back with a photo album.

"I know. Old-school, right?" he says when he sees the face I'm making. "Phone cameras were still pretty new. We couldn't afford a good one when you were small."

He sets the album on the table and flips it open. There's my mom holding me as a baby. Her smile and the look in her eyes suggest she was happy. Her brown hair and fair skin remind me that I'm a mix of white and Asian.

I squirm as we flip through lots of embarrassing baby pictures of me. But Dad and Mom looked in love. Our family looked happy.

Dad stops on a picture where Mom is pushing me on a swing.

"This is the last picture I have of the two of you," he says. "You were three. I didn't understand what was happening."

Serena squeezes his shoulder. "None of us did, Felix."

"She worked at that furniture restoration business on

Juanita Drive." Lonny pulls up the business on his phone to show me. "She searched for antiques and gave them a new life. Like I said, very talented. But then she started saying and doing things that didn't make sense."

Grippy twists my insides. "Like what?"

"She started telling everyone a popular antiques magazine was doing a cover feature about her," he says. "What she described didn't add up. And there was no evidence it was true."

Serena takes my shaking hands and squeezes. "The smallest things started setting her off. A word, or a look. She took everything the wrong way. She got angry, picked arguments, and accused people of trying to sabotage her becoming famous."

Dad wipes his eyes. "It was like another person took over her body."

He hesitates. I nod to let him know it's okay. "I know. It's like what happened with me."

"I didn't know much about mental illness then. I thought it had something to do with hormones," Dad admits.

"Did she end up in the hospital?" I ask.

Dad nods. "She was in there a long time. You were so confused about where your mommy was. That was a rough, rough time."

Serena combs her fingers through my hair. "Sweet boy. We tried to keep you busy and promised she'd be home soon. You colored pictures for Felix to take to the hospital."

"Same place as me?" I ask.

Dad pinches his lips together, but finally answers. "Yep. Same place."

"Maybe we can get a family plan next time," I quip.

They all look shocked.

"Sorry. Too dark?" I ask.

Serena sighs. "Whatever helps you cope, I suppose."

"She looked a lot better when she came home," Dad continues. "But then she dropped a bomb. She wanted to move back to her family to get their help."

Dad's tears are raw, like it happened yesterday.

"Your dad begged her to stay," Lonny says. "And we'd

become her family too. We wanted to support her. And she had you filling her with love and joy each and every day."

My body can't sit still any longer. I stand up and start a path around the room. "Not enough love and joy for her to stay. She abandoned me. *Us.* How could she do that?"

"It's complicated, Kai," Dad says. "At first, moving across the country was only temporary, until she knew she had a handle on things. But the longer she stayed away, the more she didn't want to come back."

Lonny starts cleaning up our game table. I guess I messed up another tradition.

"When she gave me full custody of you, it was from a place of love," Dad says. "I know that might be hard to understand. I didn't agree with it at the time. I wanted her to stay in your life. I've kept her in the loop, sending pictures and updates."

I help Lonny put things away. A new thought occurs to me now that I'm figuring out more about this condition.

"Did my news affect her? Like, stress her out so much that her own symptoms got triggered?" I ask.

Dad groans. "Good question. She hasn't said anything. I hope not."

Lonny and Serena bundle up to leave.

"You think you're off the hook from me taking all your money," Lonny says. "No way. Rematch."

"Heck yeah, we're doing this again," Serena adds while hugging me goodbye. "Did asking about your mom help?"

Did it? I think so. "I guess. Filling in the blanks has to be a good thing, right?"

She kisses me on the cheek. Lonny slugs my arm, and they disappear into the frosty night.

Dad's quiet while we finish straightening up. One more question weighs on my mind.

"Can you ask Mom if she wants to be in touch?" I ask. "With me. Directly."

Dad doesn't say anything for a while. "I did bring that idea up before, didn't I? Okay. I'll ask her."

He's got more to say, but he's holding it back.

"What is it?" I push.

"I don't want you to be hurt if she says no or it doesn't

go as you hope," he says. "I'm worried that could trigger your own symptoms. I wasn't thinking about that earlier."

That's a fair point.

"I'll try to keep my expectations in check," I promise.

"You've seemed low the last few days. That worries me," Dad says while we turn off the lights.

I am still low. But the weight lifted a bit tonight.

"This helped some. I'm glad I asked about her. And now this makes more sense." I point at the antique cabinet holding extra dishes and knickknacks. "I never understood why we have something so fancy."

He chuckles, and we say goodnight.

CHAPTER 15

Dad's already up and ready for work when I walk into the kitchen. The roast of his coffee smells good. I pour a little into a mug.

"Rough night?" he asks.

"Nope. I just want the taste," I say. "Don't fall down in shock, but I slept the whole night. It felt amazing."

He pretends to stumble backward.

"Voices?" he asks.

"Nothing. They're still sleeping."

"Edginess level?"

"Maybe a five."

"Okay, I'll keep my distance," he jokes. I smile.

We do the morning meds routine before he takes off. I nod when he waves his phone at me. It's shorthand to say I should call him if I need anything. He'll always answer.

After my shower, I decide today is the day I'll finish

tackling the chaos in my room. Dealing with the mess means realizing how sick I got. But I need things back the way I like them. The way I like them when I'm not super sick, I guess.

I'm still deep in the cleanup when Serena appears in the doorway. She's here to do my lunchtime med.

"Wow! I can see the floor," she cries.

She helps me bag up the stacks of notebook papers for recycling. Pages and pages of food truck sketches and lists. I've set aside the ones that make sense.

My auntie pulls out a Thanksgiving shopping list while we eat the coconut curry soup she brought. I grab my tablet and look up the recipes I plan to make. Usually, I'd wing it. But I still don't trust my mind a hundred percent. It's better to not screw up a family holiday meal.

Dad gets home right before dark. We scramble out the door for a quick walk. A new routine of ours. A bitter wind slaps our faces.

I ease into what's on my mind. "I've been thinking. What

if I go back to school after the holiday? At least then I can get into the groove a bit before winter break."

His face says this idea makes him nervous. "The school said you could start making up assignments when you feel ready. But now that it's pretty late in the semester, I'm not sure that's going to work."

Grippy tugs on my insides. "Chaz is going to fill my spot with someone else. I need to get back into things."

We circle around so the wind is at our backs. Now it howls in our ears.

"Two thoughts," he says. "Let's do the upcoming appointment with Dr. Chu and Hunter first to see what they think. And why don't you call Mrs. Rosembert to talk it through?"

Mrs. Rosembert. I can't avoid her forever. The logical part of me knows she'll understand what went on. But I'm still embarrassed about the phone call I made to her.

"I'd rather we sort through this while you're in a safe space, at home, where it's less stressful," Dad says.

Back inside, the warmth thaws our faces. Dad flips on the news, then looks in the fridge. I pace around, trying to chase away the nerves eating at my insides.

"Looks like leftovers tonight," he says. "Or do you want to whip us up something and practice getting your head back in the game? I could time you."

That's a good idea. How do I know I'm ready for the pressures of a busy restaurant if I don't test myself?

"You're feeling brave," I say.

He chuckles and searches for mystery ingredients, shooting me evil grins at times.

"Go ahead," I laugh. "You're eating whatever I make."

Dad shoos me to the living room. When he calls me back to the kitchen, the old basket we use for this game sits on the counter. I grin and step toward it.

"You have thirty minutes, chef," he says. "Open your basket."

I pull off the dish towel covering the top.

Salami.

Peanut butter.

Kale.

Horchata.

Oh man. He isn't going easy on me. My mind races through possibilities. Maybe a sauce with the peanut butter and the milky horchata drink? Wilt the kale in the sauce? The salami is the wild card. How the heck do I make that fit in?

Dad pulls me out of my thoughts. "The clock starts now."

I grab some skillets and get to work.

Dad goes easy on me about the actual time, since my shaking hands and cluttered brain slow me down. But he doesn't turn green when he eats my dinner creation. I made the salami into toasted sliders topped with my peanut-cinnamon white sauce. A weird flavor combination that somehow works.

The challenge showed that I'm rusty. But I'm not out-of-this-universe rusty.

After another good night's sleep, I fight my nerves and finally call Mrs. Rosembert.

It's afternoon when she returns my message.

"Grasshopper." Her voice and that name drag up tears I didn't know were lying in wait.

"Yoda," I say.

"Missing you, my friend. Tell me how you're doing," she says.

"Better," I say. "I'm sorry."

It's all I can get out.

"No sorry. Let's figure out your next step, okay?"

We talk for a long time about my options. How she'll be able to help me reach my goals if I come back. And if I don't.

If I don't come back. That's the fear I've been trying to ignore.

"I'm blowing it with Chaz," I share. "This was my chance."

"No, this was *one* chance," she corrects me. "Of many. And how do you think that chance will work out if you try being in a pressure cooker kitchen while unstable? The bistro, or another restaurant in the program, will take you when you're ready."

Ready. What does that mean for me now? It's like I can't trust my brain to tell me the truth. How will I be able to trust it to know when I'm ready?

"Lots of people have medical issues that need extra care," she says. "Sometimes that involves taking breaks or doubling down to focus on their health. It can feel like the end of the world, but it's not. And there's no shame in it."

We talk until she has to leave. She's the first person besides my family and clinical team I've talked to in weeks. I trust her to be real with me. I trust Krissie to do that too. I decide to call her, but it's late on Friday afternoon. I'll call her next week.

It's Friday. I wonder if my friends are getting together tonight. I'd rather not know yet. But they've been on my mind. Maybe Ian and Josie didn't actually abandon me like I thought. That's what Dad insists.

Still, it feels like we lost our magic. What if we can't get it back?

There *is* someone I trust to help me sort through it. Now that my mind is clearing, I realize he's been a steady friend. Grippy unleashes zombie butterflies as I worry about whether this will still be true. But I text Gavin, telling him I'm ready to talk.

CHAPTER 16

Dad nudges me awake when we reach the clinic. I try to shake off the grogginess. We head in for our appointment with Dr. Chu and Hunter.

"I hate being around these sick people," the man says.

He's not real, I remind myself. I haven't heard the girl for a while. But the man won't leave me alone for long.

Hunter walks with us to Dr. Chu's office, talking with Dad about Thanksgiving plans. Inside the office, we settle in. Dr. Chu studies me with a smile.

"Will you be doing most of the cooking this week?" he asks.

"I hope so. At least that's the plan," I say. "If I feel up to it."

We talk about menus. Then he asks me about my sleep, my mood, and my hallucinations. How I'm getting along with other people.

"I felt a lot better last week," I share. "But it's like I went backward this weekend. It was hard to sleep. I'm jumping out of my skin. The voices are back. Well, one voice."

"Any triggers you can think of?" he asks.

Dad and I look at each other.

"He's stressing about his mom," Dad says finally. "He wants to be in touch. She isn't sure yet. Maybe that's triggering symptoms?"

Dr. Chu makes a sympathetic *ahhhh* sound. "That sounds hard. What do you think, Kai?"

What do I think? That I'm in a battle with my body and my brain. "I'm trying to not think about her. And not get too upset while I wait for an answer. Obviously, I'm failing. But how do you know if something is really causing symptoms?"

"Good question," he says. "We don't always know. Sometimes it's guesswork. Sometimes we can remove the suspected trigger and see if that helps. Like having you stay home to reset. But that's not going to be easy in this case."

Hunter jumps in. "It's hard when we're in a waiting game for something, not sure what's going to happen. We can work on some coping methods around this if you want."

I nod slowly. "But besides what's happening with my mom, I'm doing what you said to do. Am I getting better or not?"

"You're looking a lot better," Hunter says. "But it might not be a smooth path, even when there aren't triggers."

Dr. Chu asks Dad what he's seeing.

Dad gives me a big smile and squeezes my arm. "Lots of progress. No paranoia. He's sleeping well more nights. He's calmer. Able to focus more. He's even getting back into our kitchen to cook some." He keeps his hand on my arm. "And the side effects of the meds seem less intense now. Do you agree?"

I nod. It's good to hear him sounding less worried. But then he brings up school. That does have him worried.

"How do you feel about school, Kai?" Dr. Chu asks.

In the moments when I'm honest with myself, it has

me worried too. "I've fallen apart twice in front of people. I feel stuck. If I go back and it's too much, I'm now officially the boy who went crazy. If I don't go back, my future is in the toilet. How would *you* be feeling?"

Everyone's quiet. Dad hangs his head and takes a deep breath.

"Unfortunately, there is still a lot of stigma around mental illness," Dr. Chu finally says. "I don't like the word *crazy* because it's used as an insult. Let's focus on how to help you instead of how to fix society."

Hunter grabs a folder from a side table. It's for the early intervention program. "Ready to consider it again?"

There's that word. *Ready.*

"Can't trust them," the man says. "Let's go."

But I look at Dad and take the folder this time. Maybe this is what I need if this illness is going to be part of my life. I've got to save my goals. And my relationships. It sounds like Mom getting sick nearly broke Dad. And now it's happening all over again. Maybe this program can help us both.

We stop at a coffee shop on the way home. I know it's a test to see how I do in a noisy place and around people. The clanking dishes and buzz of conversations bump up my blood pressure. There's the answer.

Dad emails the school that afternoon. It turns out he'd already looked up the details. He knew how to get the ball rolling.

Me: *Hey, made a big decision today*

Gavin: *Details, please*

Me: *Switching to online school for now. And doing that program my clinic team keeps bringing up*

Gavin: *Wow. Two big decisions. How you feeling?*

Me: *Not sure. All the feels, wrapped into a stale burrito*

Gavin: *Don't make me one of those!*

Me: *Order up*

Gavin: *You've got this*

Me: *We'll see. Where you at?*

Gavin: *Library. Saw Krissie today. She asked about you*

Me: *Been wanting to call her*

Gavin: *Think she'd like that*

I'm browsing through the online school program website when Krissie returns my call.

She sings my name. "How I've missed my lunchtime buddy."

"Same," I say.

"Well? How are you feeling?"

I make her laugh with my "sweet as honey" answer.

"You were as sour as an unripe blackberry last time I saw you," she says.

"Yeah, sorry about that."

"Don't be. I'm joking," she says. "We knew you might have some ups and downs at first."

I tell her about my big decisions. We still need to talk to Mrs. Rosembert, but it looks like I can keep doing the food lab classes on-site. And the recovery program will help me get settled into the job training—or even a job—when I'm ready.

"You know what? Props for focusing on your health," she says. "This is a condition that you can't ignore in hopes it just goes away. It's smart to take some time to get a better handle on it."

Krissie makes me promise to visit when I'm on campus. "And I won't be mad if you bring me a tasty Kai Lum creation now and then."

That night, sleep comes fast and easy. Exactly the medicine I need.

CHAPTER 17

I dump my winter gear in the hallway. Leftover snow from my boots melts into puddles on the mat. My group session ran over, and now I'm behind. Good thing I did most of the prep work this morning.

I'm putting the rice in the cooker when Dad stomps in from the brutal cold. He puts his icy hands on my neck.

"No!" I scream and laugh.

"Weather like this makes me want to move back to the island," he says. "How can I help?"

I grab a mug and fill it with the hot cider that's been simmering all day in the crockpot. "You've had a long day at work, honey. Take this and go relax."

He chuckles at our longtime joke but doesn't move.

"I've got this," I say.

"I know you do. I'm just enjoying the moment," he says before heading to the living room.

My shrimp is prepped and I'm working on the salmon when the doorbell rings. More boot stomps. Voices and a current of chilly wind drift into the kitchen.

"Hey, man. I am so hungry," Gavin says when he joins me.

"Good." I hand him a mug of cider and set him up with salad fixings to toss.

We work in silence for a bit. Not awkward. There's always been an easy rhythm to our friendship.

I glaze the salmon with miso and get it in the oven. Then I begin sautéing the shrimp. "Done with finals?"

"Yep. I need to catch up on sleep over the break."

"It's the best medicine!" I joke.

He turns the salad over to me. "I'm going to hang out with Ian and Josie next week. Want to join us?"

Now our silence turns uncomfortable.

"Like I said before, they want to get back to how things were," Gavin says gently. "They miss you."

"I miss them too. But I'm worried we can't get back to how it was," I say. "I'm different now. It's all different now."

Gavin sighs. "Yeah, I get that. But we're still a tight group of friends. It's like you were deployed to another place for a while. We saved your spot, and now you're back. Even if you have to redeploy later, your spot isn't going away."

"Let me think about it," I answer. "I need to be in the right headspace."

He accepts that with a nod.

I refill his mug and steer him out of the kitchen. "Go hang out with Dad. I'll have the meal out soon."

A whisper distracts me while I'm finishing up. Too faint to know whether it's the girl or the man. *Yeah*, I say in my head. *I know you're still here. But I'm not feeding you.*

When I bring the dishes to the table, Gavin and Dad grin at each other. We do a holiday toast and dig in.

"I was at one of the wineries today talking through their food order for the new year," Dad tells me. "They're updating their menu. It made me hungry just hearing it. And it made me happy thinking about all the possibilities ahead for you once your training is done."

Gavin toasts to that idea. "To Chef Lum!"

"And to the professor," I toast back. "The smartest guy around when it comes to rocks!"

"What's the latest on the romance front?" Dad asks Gavin. "Last we talked, there was a girl on your radar."

My best friend turns tomato red. "Yeah, we talked more, and I finally asked her out."

We wait, excited to know what she said.

"She said yes." He grins. "We're going out this weekend."

We toast that too.

I'll get the details from him later, away from Dad's overeager ears.

They both put more helpings on their plates. That's a good sign. It means I've still got the touch.

"How was group today?" Dad asks.

"Hilarious," I answer.

They shoot me worried looks.

"Our therapist is really into plaid clothes," I explain. "Totally over the top. We call him Tartan Man. So, we all wore as much plaid as we could today. It looked like a Scottish lumberjack convention."

They take in my flannel shirt, and I show them my plaid socks. I smile as they laugh.

We clear the table, and I bring out dessert. "Coconut cream pie with a macadamia nut crust," I announce. "You better like it. Not the fastest dish to make."

"No worries there," Dad says. "It's like a slice of home."

I slip into the kitchen and bring back a second small dish with the top covered. "This special treat is for me."

"No fair," Gavin complains. Then he sees what I brought out.

Under the towel is a slice of bread spread with brown, sticky, yeasty Marmite. "This, my friend, is for breaking my promise."

"What promise?" Gavin and Dad ask over each other.

"About my meds," I explain. "I did a friend pledge to keep taking them. Then I broke that in record time."

Gavin pokes at my choice of a gross food with his fork. "You did indeed promise me that. Hopefully we're past that now."

"I'm doing my best. I don't love the meds, but I know they're keeping my mind clear."

Dad toasts that. What a year. But we're about to turn the calendar. And I've got options ahead. That's enough to keep me going.

"Dig in, Lummy," Gavin says, grinning.

And so, I do.

ABOUT THE AUTHOR

Jennifer Phillips writes stories that celebrate creativity, courage, and determination. She started out as a newspaper reporter in the Midwest and then spent many years in corporate and nonprofit communications. Now she splits her professional energy between writing for children and helping grown-ups make things work better through process improvement and creativity methods. She also advocates for social justice needs, especially concerning disability and mental illness. A Seattle mom of two young adult girls and one bird, she has more story ideas than time. She does her best writing super early in the morning when the coffee is piping hot and the house extremely quiet. Come visit her at jenniferphillipsauthor.com.

TURN THE PAGE TO DISCOVER MORE EXCITING HORIZON TITLES!

CHECK OUT OTHER HORIZON FICTION TITLES!

HORIZON

FIREBIRD CAGED

MAYA CHHABRA

Ashley didn't mean to get pregnant her senior year in high school. She didn't mean to scare her hardworking and financially struggling mom, or to hide the truth from her awkward ex, Danny. She also didn't mean to illegally take her well-off friend Madi's prescription Xanax to cope with the stress—and she definitely didn't mean to do it more than once.

When a doctor reports Ashley to the State of Wisconsin as a drug-addicted threat to her own unborn child, she is forcibly detained under the obscure and secretive Act 292 civil detention system for pregnant women, stranded in the county juvenile shelter home, and stigmatized by authorities who assign her fetus a lawyer but not her. It's a struggle for Ashley just to get medical care for the pregnancy supposedly being protected—never mind fighting for her own freedom and making sure her baby isn't taken away by social services after birth. Who's going to protect Ashley herself?

But Ashley is stronger than anyone knows, and she has allies on the outside who believe in her. This is a fight Ashley can win—but only if she stops drifting passively, starts believing in herself, and chooses not to give in to despair.

CHECK OUT OTHER HORIZON FICTION TITLES!

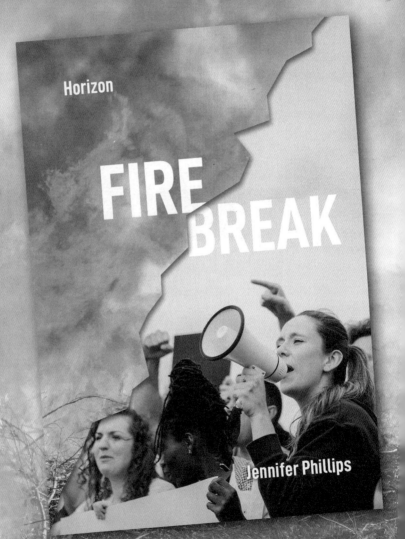

Horizon

FIRE
BREAK

Jennifer Phillips

High school junior Alia is good at sports but struggles with schoolwork, hindered by her learning disabilities. The latest history assignment on genocide is just more homework to be endured. That's until a troubling conversation with her beloved grandmother reluctantly jolts Alia into action. Between the country's shifting mood toward the elderly and new government programs championed as practical ways to deal with a burgeoning elderly population, Alia fears that senior citizens are being targeted for something more ominous. To rally others and challenge the growing oppression, Alia will need to step up and speak out. But people tend to doubt Alia due to her learning difficulties. Can she get people to listen to her? More importantly, can she believe in herself?